Harry Harrison was born in Stamford, Connecticut, in 1925 and lived in New York City until 1943, when he joined the United States Army. He was a machine-gun instructor during the war, but returned to his art studies after leaving the army.

Apart from enjoying an enviable reputation as one of the best writers on the science fiction scene, Harry Harrison is a well travelled man of wide interests and accomplishments. A first-class short story writer, an experienced editor and anthologist, a translator, a trained cartoonist, he has also been a commercial illustrator, an art director, an hydraulic press operator, a truck driver, and is, of course, a first-rate novelist.

Harrison's style leaps from the humour of his *Stainless Steel Rat* novels, to purist sf, to the splendid combination of fantasy and science fiction as found in *Captive Universe*.

Deathworld 2

HARRY HARRISON

All Nature is but Art, unknown to thee;
All Chance, Direction, which thou canst not see;
All Discord, Harmony not understood;
All partial Evil, universal Good:
And, spite of Pride, in erring Reason's spite,
One truth is clear, WHATEVER IS, IS RIGHT.

–Alexander Pope, *An Essay on Man*

SPHERE BOOKS LIMITED
30/32 Gray's Inn Road, London WC1X 8JL

First published (under the title *The Ethical Engineer*)
in Great Britain by Victor Gollancz Ltd 1964
Copyright © Harry Harrison 1964
Published by Sphere Books 1973
Reprinted May 1974

For John W. Campbell
without whose aid this book –
and a good percentage of modern science fiction –
would never have been written

TRADE
MARK

Set in Intertype Plantin

Printed in Great Britain by
Hazell Watson & Viney Ltd
Aylesbury, Bucks

ISBN 0 7221 4374 5

CHAPTER ONE

"Just a moment," Jason said into the phone, then turned away for a moment and shot an attacking horndevil. "No, I'm not doing anything important. I'll come over now and maybe I can help."

He switched off the phone and the radio operator's image faded from the screen. When he passed the gutted horndevil it stirred with a last spark of vicious life, and its horn clattered on his flexible metal boot; he kicked the body off the wall into the jungle below.

It was dark in the perimeter guard turret; the only illumination came from the flickering lights of the defense screen controls. Meta looked up swiftly at him and smiled, then turned her full attention back to the alarm board.

"I'm going over to the spaceport radio tower," Jason told her. "There is a spacer in orbit, trying to make contact in an unknown language. Maybe I can help."

"Hurry back," Meta said and, after a rapid check that all her alarms were in the green, she turned in the chair and reached up to him. Her arms held him, slim-muscled and as strong as a man's, but her lips were warm, feminine. He returned the kiss, though she broke away as suddenly as she had begun, turning her attention back to the alarm and defense system.

"That's the trouble with Pyrrus," Jason said. "Too much efficiency." He bent over and gave her a small bite on the nape of the neck and she laughed and slapped at him playfully without taking her eyes from the alarms. He moved —but not fast enough—and went out rubbing his bruised ear. "Lady weight-lifter!" he muttered under his breath.

The radio operator was alone in the spaceport tower, a teen-age boy who had never been offplanet, and therefore knew only Pyrran, while Jason, after his career as a professional gambler, spoke or had nodding acquaintance with most of the galactic languages.

"It's orbiting out of range now," the operator said. "Be back in a moment. Talks something different." He turned the gain up, and above the crackle of atmospherics a voice slowly grew.

"... *jeg kan ikke forstå* ... *Pyrrus, kan dig hør mig* ...?"

"No trouble with that," Jason said, reaching for the microphone. "It's Nytdansk—they speak it on most of the planets in the Polaris area." He thumbed the switch on.

"*Pyrrus til rumfartskib*, over," he said, and opened the switch. The answer came back in the same language.

"Request landing permission. What are your coordinates?"

"Permission denied, and the suggestion strongly presented that you find a healthier planet."

"That is impossible, since I have a message for Jason dinAlt and I have information that he is here."

Jason looked at the crackling loudspeaker with new interest. "Your information is correct : dinAlt speaking. What is the message?"

"It cannot be delivered over a public circuit. I am now following your radio beam down. Will you give me instructions?"

"You do realize that you are probably committing suicide? This is the deadliest planet in the galaxy, and all the life forms, from the bacteria up to the clawhawks—which are as big as the ship you're flying—are inimical to man. There is a truce of sorts going now, but it is still certain death for an outworlder like you. Can you hear me?"

There was no answer. Jason shrugged and looked at the approach radar.

"Well, it's your life. But don't say with your dying breath that you weren't warned. I'll bring you in—but only if you agree to stay in your ship. I'll come out to you; that way you have a fifty-fifty chance that the decontamination cycling in your spacelock will kill the local microscopic life."

"That is agreeable," came the answer, "since I have no wish to die—only to deliver my message."

Jason guided the ship in, watched it emerge from the low-lying clouds, hover, then drop stern first with a grating crash. The shock absorbers took up most of the blow, but the ship had bent a support and stood at a decided angle.

"Terrible landing," the radio operator grunted, and turned back to his controls, uninterested in the stranger. Pyrrans have no casual curiosity.

Jason was the direct opposite. Curiosity had brought him to Pyrrus, involved him in the planet-wide war, and almost killed him. Now curiosity drove him towards the ship. He hesitated a moment as he realized that the radio operator had not understood his conversation with the strange pilot, and could not know that he planned to enter the ship. If he was walking into trouble he could expect no help.

"I can take care of myself," he said to himself with a laugh, and when he raised his hand his gun leaped out of the power holster strapped to the inside of his wrist and slammed into his hand. His index finger was already contracted, and when the guardless trigger hit it a single shot banged out, blasting the distant dartweed he had aimed at.

He was good, and he knew it. He would never be as good as the native Pyrrans, born and raised on this deadly planet, with its double gravity, but he was faster and more deadly than any offworlder could possibly be. He could handle any trouble that might develop—and he expected trouble. In the past he had had many differences of opinion with the police and various other planetary authorities, though he could think of none of them who would bother to send police across interstellar space to arrest him.

Why had this ship come?

There was an identification number painted on the spacer's stern, and a rather familiar heraldic device. Where had he seen that before?

His attention was distracted by the opening of the outer door of the airlock and he stepped inside. Once it had sealed behind him, he closed his eyes while the supersonics and ultraviolet of the decon cycle did their best to eliminate the various minor life forms that had come in on his clothes. They finally finished, and when the inner door began to open he pressed tight against it, ready to jump through as soon as it had opened wide enough. If there were any surprises he wanted them to be his.

When he went through the door he realized he was falling. His gun sprang into his hand and he had it half raised towards the man in the spacesuit who sat in the control chair.

"Gas . . ." was all he managed to say, and he was out before he hit the metal deck.

Consciousness returned, accompanied by a thudding headache that made Jason wince when he moved, and when he opened his eyes the pain of the light made him screw them shut again. Whatever the drug was that had knocked him

7

out, it was fast-working, and seemed to be oxidized just as quickly. The headache faded to a dull throb, and he could open his eyes without feeling that needles were being driven into them.

He was seated in a standard space-chair that had been equipped with wrist and ankle locks, which were now well secured. A man sat in the chair next to him, intent on the spaceship's controls; the ship was in flight and well into space. The stranger was working the computer, cutting a tape to control their flight in jump space.

Jason took the opportunity to study the man. He seemed to be a little old for a policeman, though on second thought it was really hard to be sure of his age. His hair was grey and cropped so short it was like a skullcap, but the wrinkles in his leathery skin seemed to have been caused more by exposure than by advanced years. Tall and firmly erect, he appeared underweight at first glance, until Jason realized this effect was caused by the total absence of any excess flesh. It was as though he had been cooked by the sun and leached by the rain until only bone, tendon, and muscle were left. When he moved his head the muscles stood out like cables under the skin of his neck and his hands at the controls were like the browned talons of some bird. A hard finger pressed the switch that activated the jump control, and he turned away from the board to face Jason.

"I see you are awake. It was a mild gas. I did not enjoy using it, but it was the safest way."

When he talked his jaw opened and shut with the no-nonsense seriousness of a bank vault. His deepset, cold blue eyes stared fixedly from under thick dark brows. There was not the slightest element of humor in his expression or in his words.

"Not a very friendly thing to do," Jason said, while he quietly tested the restraining bands. They were locked and tight. "If I had any idea that your important personal message was going to be a dose of knock-out gas I might have thought twice about guiding you in for a landing."

"Deceit for the deceitful," the snapping-turtle mouth bit out. "Had there been any other way to capture you, I would have used it. But considering your reputation as a ruthless killer, and the undoubted fact that you have friends on Pyrrus, I took you in the only manner possible."

"Very noble of you, I'm sure." Jason was getting angry at

8

the other's uncompromising self-righteousness. "The end justifies the means and all that—not exactly an original argument. But I walked in with my eyes open and I'm not complaining." Not much, he thought bitterly. The next best thing to kicking this crumb around the block would be kicking himself for being so stupid. "But if it's not asking too much, would you mind telling me who you are and just why you have gone to all this trouble to obtain my under-nourished body."

"I am Mikah Samon. I am returning you to Cassylia for trial and sentencing."

"Cassylia—I thought I recognized the identification on this ship. I suppose I shouldn't be surprised to hear that they are still interested in finding me. But you ought to know that there is very little remaining of the three billion, seventeen million credits that I won from your casino."

"Cassylia does not want the money back," Mikah said as he locked the controls and swung about in his chair. "They do not want you back either, since you are their planetary hero now. When you escaped with your ill-gotten gains they realized that they would never see the money again. So they put their propaganda mills to work and you are now known throughout all the adjoining star systems as 'Jason Three-Billion', the living proof of the honesty of their dishonest games, and a lure for all the weak in spirit. You tempt them into gambling for money instead of working honestly for it."

"Pardon me for being slow-witted today," Jason said, shaking his head rapidly to loosen up the stuck synapses. "I'm having a little difficulty in following you. What kind of a policeman are you, to arrest me for trial after the charges have been dropped?"

"I am not a policeman," Mikah said sternly, his long fingers woven tightly together before him, his eyes wide and penetrating. "I am a believer in Truth—nothing more. The corrupt politicians who control Cassylia have placed you on a pedestal of honor. Honoring you, another and—if possible—a more corrupt man, and behind your image they have waxed fat. But I am going to use the Truth to destroy that image, and when I destroy the image I shall destroy the evil that produced it."

"That's a tall order for one man," Jason said calmly—more calmly than he really felt. "Do you have a cigarette?"

"There is of course no tobacco or spirits on this ship. And I am more than one man—I have followers. The Truth Party is already a power to be reckoned with. We have spent much time and energy in tracking you down, but it was worth it. We have followed your dishonest trail into the past, to Mahaut's Planet, to the Nebula Casino on Galipto, through a series of sordid crimes that turn an honest man's stomach. We have warrants for your arrest from each of these places, in some cases even the results of trials and your death sentence."

"I suppose it doesn't bother your sense of legality that those trials were all held in my absence?" Jason asked. "Or that I have only fleeced sacinos and gamblers—who make their living by fleecing suckers?"

Mikah Samon wiped away this consideration with a wave of his hand. "You have been proved guilty of a number of crimes. No amount of wriggling on the hook can change that. You should be thankful that your revolting record will have a good use in the end. It will be the lever with which we shall topple the grafting government of Cassylia."

"I'm going to have to do something about that curiosity of mine," Jason said. "Look at me now"— He rattled his wrists in their restraining bands and the servo motors whined a bit as the detector unit came to life and tightened the grasp of the cuffs, limiting his movement. "A little while ago I was enjoying my health and freedom when they called me to talk to you on the radio. Then, instead of letting you plow into the side of a hill, I guide you in for a landing, and can't resist the impulse to poke my stupid head into your baited trap. I'm going to have to learn to fight those impulses."

"If that is supposed to be a plea for mercy, it is sickening," Mikah said. "I have never taken favors, nor do I owe anything to men of your type. Nor will I ever."

"*Ever*, like *never*, is a long time," Jason said very quietly. "I wish I had your peace of mind about the sure order of things."

"Your remark shows that there might be hope for you yet. You might be able to recognize the Truth before you die. I will help you, talk to you, and explain."

"Better the execution," Jason said chokingly.

CHAPTER TWO

"Are you going to feed me by hand—or unlock my wrists while I eat?" Jason asked. Mikah stood over him with the tray, undecided. Jason gave a verbal prod, very gently, because whatever else he was, Mikah was not stupid. "I would prefer you to feed me, of course—you'd make an excellent body servant."

"You are capable of eating by yourself," Mikah responded instantly, sliding the tray into the slots of Jason's chair. "But you will have to do it with only one hand, since if you were freed you would only cause trouble." He touched the control on the back of the chair and the right wrist lock snapped open. Jason stretched his cramped fingers and picked up the fork.

While he ate, Jason's eyes were busy. Not obviously, for a gambler's attention is never obvious, but many things can be seen if you keep your eyes open and your attention apparently elsewhere : a sudden glimpse of someone's cards, the slight change of expression that reveals a player's strength. Item by item, his seemingly random glance touched the contents of the cabin. Control console, screens, computer, chart screen, jump control, chart case, bookshelf. Everything was observed, considered, and remembered. Some combination of them would fit into the plan.

So far, all he had was the beginning and the end of an idea. Beginning : He was a prisoner in this ship, on his way back to Cassylia. End : He was not going to remain a prisoner—nor return to Cassylia. Now all that was missing was the vital middle. The end seemed impossible at the moment, but Jason never considered that it couldn't be done. He operated on the principle that you made your own luck. You kept your eyes open as things evolved, and at the right moment you acted. If you acted fast enough, that was good luck. If you worried over the possibilities until the moment had passed, that was bad luck.

He pushed the empty plate away and stirred sugar into his cup. Mikah had eaten sparingly and was now starting on his second cup of tea. His eyes were fixed, unfocused in thought as he drank. He started slightly when Jason spoke to him.

"Since you don't stock cigarettes on this ship, how about letting me smoke my own? You'll have to dig them out for me, since I can't reach the pocket while I'm chained to this chair."

"I cannot help you," Mikah said, not moving. "Tobacco is an irritant, a drug, and a carcinogen. If I gave you a cigarette I would be giving you cancer."

"Don't be a hypocrite!" Jason snapped, inwardly pleased at the rewarding flush in the other's neck. "They've taken the cancer-producing agents out of tobacco for centuries now. And if they hadn't—how does that affect this situation? You're taking me to Cassylia to certain death. So why should you concern yourself with the state of my lungs in the future?"

"I had not considered it that way. It is just that there are certain rules of life—"

"Are there?" Jason broke in, keeping the initiative and the advantage. "Not as many as you like to think. And you people who are always dreaming up the rules never carry your thinking far enough. You are against drugs. Which drugs? What about the tannic acid in that tea you're drinking? Or the caffeine in it? It's loaded with caffeine—a drug that is both a strong stimulant and a diuretic. That's why you won't find tea in spacesuit canteens. That's a case of a drug forbidden for a good reason. Can you justify your cigarette ban the same way?"

Mikah was about to speak, then thought for a moment. "Perhaps you are right. I am tired, and it is not important." He warily took the cigarette case from Jason's pocket and dropped it onto the tray. Jason didn't attempt to interfere. Mikah poured himself a third cup of tea with a slightly apologetic air.

"You must excuse me, Jason, for attempting to make you conform to my own standards. When you are in pursuit of the big Truths, you sometimes let the little Truths slip. I am not intolerant, but I do tend to expect everyone else to live up to certain criteria I have set for myself. Humility is something we should never forget, and I thank you for reminding me of it. The search for Truth is hard."

"There is no Truth," Jason told him, the anger and insult gone now from his voice, since he wanted to keep his captor involved in the conversation. Involved enough to forget about the free wrist for a while. He raised the cup to his lips

12

and let the tea touch his lips without drinking any. The half-full cup supplied an unconsidered reason for his free hand.

"No Truth?" Mikah weighed the thought. "You can't possibly mean that. The galaxy is filled with Truth; it's the touchstone of Life itself. It's the thing that separates Mankind from the animals."

"There is no Truth, no Life, no Mankind. At least not the way you spell them—with capital letters. They don't exist."

Mikah's taut skin contracted into a furrow of concentration. "You will have to explain yourself," he said. "For you are not being clear."

"I'm afraid it's you who aren't being clear. You're making a reality where none exists. Truth—with a small *t*—is a description, a relationship. A way to describe a statement. A semantic tool. But Truth with a capital *T* is an imaginary word, a noise with no meaning. It pretends to be a noun, but it has no referent. It stands for nothing. It means nothing. When you say, 'I believe in Truth,' you are really saying, 'I believe in nothing.'"

"You are incredibly wrong!" Mikah said, leaning forward, stabbing with his finger. "Truth is a philosophical abstraction, one of the tools that our minds have used to raise us above the beasts—the proof that we are not beasts ourselves, but a higher order of creation. Beasts can be true—but they cannot know Truth. Beasts can see, but they cannot see Beauty."

"Arrgh!" Jason growled. "It's impossible to talk to you, much less enjoy any comprehensible exchange of ideas. We aren't even speaking the same language. Forgetting for the moment who is right and who is wrong, we should go back to basics and at least agree on the meaning of the terms that we are using. To begin with—can you define the difference between *ethics* and *ethos*?"

"Of course," Mikah snapped, a glint of pleasure in his eyes at the thought of a good rousing round of hair-splitting. "Ethics is the discipline dealing with what is good or bad, or right and wrong—or with moral duty and obligation. Ethos means the guiding beliefs, standards, or ideals that characterize a group or community."

"Very good. I can see that you have been spending the long spaceship nights with your nose buried in the books. Now make sure the difference between those two terms is very clear, because it is the heart of the little communication

13

problem we have here. Ethos is inextricably linked with a single society and cannot be separated from it, or it loses all meaning. Do you agree?"

"Well . . ."

"Come, come—you *have* to agree on the terms of your own definition. The ethos of a group is just a catch-all term for the ways in which the members of a group rub against each other. Right?"

Mikah reluctantly gave a nod of acquiescence.

"Now that we agree about that, we can push on one step further. Ethics, again by your definition, must deal with any number of societies or groups. If there are any absolute laws of ethics, they must be so inclusive that they can be applied to *any* society. A law of ethics must be as universal of application, as is the law of gravity."

"I don't follow you. . . ."

"I didn't think you would when I got to this point. You people who prattle about your Universal Laws never really consider the exact meaning of the term. My knowledge of the history of science is a little vague, but I'm willing to bet that the first Law of Gravity ever dreamed up stated that things fell at such and such a speed, and accelerated at such and such a rate. That's not a law, but an observation that isn't even complete until you add 'on this planet'. On a planet with a different mass there will be a different observation. The *law* of gravity is the formula :

$$F = \frac{mM}{d^2}$$

and this can be used to compute the force of gravity between any two bodies anywhere. This is a way of expressing fundamental and unalterable principles that apply in all circumstances. If you are going to have any real ethical laws they will have to have this same universality. They will have to work on Cassylia or Pyrrus, or on any planet or in any society you can find. Which brings us back to you. What you so grandly call—with capital letters and a flourish of trumpets—'Laws of Ethics' aren't laws at all, but are simply little chunks of tribal ethos, aboriginal observations made by a gang of desert sheepherders to keep order in the house—or tent. These rules aren't capable of any universal application;

14

even you must see that. Just think of the different planets that you have been on, and the number of weird and wonderful ways people have of reacting to each other—then try and visualize ten rules of conduct that would be applicable in all these societies. An impossible task. Yet I'll bet that you have ten rules you want me to obey, and if one of them is wasted on an injunction against saying prayers to carved idols, I can imagine just how universal the other nine are. You aren't being ethical if you try to apply them wherever you go—you're just finding a particularly fancy way to commit suicide!"

"You are being insulting!"

"I hope so. If I can't reach you in any other way, perhaps insult will jar you out of your state of moral smugness. How dare you even consider having me tried for stealing money from the Cassylia casino, when all I was doing was conforming to their own code of ethics! They run crooked gambling games, so the law under their local ethos must be that crooked gambling is the norm. So I cheated them, conforming to their norm. If they have also passed a law that says cheating at gambling is illegal, the *law* is unethical, not the cheating. If you are bringing me back to be tried by that law you are unethical, and I am the helpless victim of an evil man."

"Limb of Satan!" Mikah shouted, leaping to his feet and pacing back and forth before Jason, clasping and unclasping his hands with agitation. "You seek to confuse me with your semantics and so-called ethics, which are simply opportunism and greed. There is a Higher Law that cannot be argued—"

"That is an impossible statement—and I can prove it." Jason pointed at the books on the wall. "I can prove it with your own books, some of that light reading on the shelf there. Not the Aquinas—too thick. But the little volume with 'Lull' on the spine. Is that Ramon Lull's *The Booke of the Ordre of Chyvalry*?"

Mikah's eyes widened. "You know the book? You're acquainted with Lull's writing?"

"Of course," Jason said, with an offhandedness he did not feel, since this was the only book in the collection he could remember reading; the odd title had stuck in his head. "Now let me see it, and I shall prove to you what I mean." There was no way to tell from the unchanged naturalness of his words that this was the moment he had been working carefully towards. He sipped the tea, none of his tenseness showing.

Mikah Samon took the book down and handed it to him.

Jason flipped through the pages while he talked. "Yes . . . yes, this is perfect. An almost ideal example of your kind of thinking. Do you like to read Lull?"

"Inspirational!" Mikah answered, his eyes shining. "There is beauty in every line, and Truths that we have forgotten in the rush of modern life. A reconciliation and proof of the interrelationship between the Mystical and the Concrete. By manipulation of symbols, he explains everything by absolute logic."

"He proves nothing about nothing," Jason said emphatically. "He plays word games. He takes a word, gives it an abstract and unreal value, then proves this value by relating it to other words with the same sort of nebulous antecedents. His facts aren't facts—they're just meaningless sounds. This is the key point where your universe and mine differ. You live in this world of meaningless facts that have no existence. My world contains facts that can be weighed, tested, proven related to other facts in a logical manner. My facts are unshakeable and unarguable. They exist."

"Show me one of your unshakeable facts," Mikah said, voice calmer now than Jason's.

"Over there," Jason said. "The large green book over the console. It contains facts that even you will agree are true— I'll eat every page if you don't. Hand it to me." He sounded angry, making overly bold statements, and Mikah fell right into the trap. He handed the volume to Jason, using both hands, for it was very thick, metal-bound, and heavy.

"Now listen closely and try and understand, even if it is difficult for you," Jason said, opening the book. Mikah smiled wryly at this assumption of his ignorance. "This is a stellar ephemeris, just as packed with facts as an egg is with meat. In some ways it is a history of mankind. Now look at the jump screen there on the control console and you will see what I mean. Do you see the horizontal green line? Well, that's our course."

"Since this is my ship and I am piloting it, I am aware of that," Mikah said. "Proceed with your proof."

"Bear with me," Jason told him. "I'll try to keep it simple. Now, the red dot on the green line is our ship's position.

The number above the screen is our next navigational point, the spot where a star's gravitational field is strong enough to be detected in jump space. The number is the star's code listing BD89-046-299. I look it up in the book"—he quickly flipped the pages—"and find its listing. No name. A row of code symbols, though, that tell a lot about it. This little symbol means that there is a planet or planets suitable for man to live on. It doesn't say, though, if any people are there."

"Where does this all lead to?" Mikah asked.

"Patience—you'll see in a moment. Now look at the screen. The green dot approaching on the course line is the PMP—Point of Maximum Proximity. When the red dot and green dot coincide . . ."

"Give me that book," Mikah ordered, stepping forward, aware suddenly that something was wrong. He was just an instant too late.

"Here's your proof," Jason said, and hurled the heavy book through the jump screen into the delicate circuits behind. Before it hit, he had thrown the second book. There was a tinkling crash, a flare of light, and the crackle of shorted circuits.

The floor gave a tremendous heave as the relays snapped open, dropping the ship through into normal space.

Mikah grunted in pain, clubbed to the floor by the suddenness of the transition. Locked in the chair, Jason fought the heaving of his stomach and the blackness before his eyes. As Mikah dragged himself to his feet, Jason took careful aim and sent the tray and dishes hurtling into the smoking ruin of the jump computer.

"There's your fact," he said in cheerful triumph. "Your incontrovertible, gold-plated, uranium-cored fact.

"We're not going to Cassylia any more!"

CHAPTER THREE

"You have killed us both," Mikah said, his face strained and white, but his voice under control.

"Not quite," Jason told him cheerily. "But I have killed the jump control so we can't get to another star. However, there's nothing wrong with our space drive, so we can make a landing on one of the planets—you saw for yourself that there is at least one suitable for habitation."

"Where I will fix the jump drive and continue the voyage to Cassylia. You will have gained nothing."

"Perhaps," Jason answered in his most noncommittal voice, for he did not have the slightest intention of continuing the trip, no matter what Mikah Samon thought.

His captor had reached the same conclusion. "Put your hand back on the chair arm," he ordered, and locked the cuff into place again. He stumbled as the drive started and the ship changed direction. "What was that?" he asked.

"Emergency control. The ship's computer knows that something drastic is wrong, so it has taken over. You can override it with the manuals, but don't bother yet. The ship can do a better job than either of us, with its senses and stored data. It will find the planet we're looking for, plot a course, and get us there with the most economy of time and fuel. When we get into the atmosphere you can take over and look for a spot to set down."

"I do not believe a word you say now," Mikah said grimly. "I am going to take control and get a call out on the emergency band. Someone will hear it."

As he started forward the ship lurched again and all the lights went out. In the darkness, flames could be seen flashing inside the controls. There was a hiss of foam and they vanished. With a weak flicker the emergency lighting circuit came on.

"I shouldn't have thrown the Ramon Lull book," Jason said. "The ship can't stomach it any more than I could."

"You are irreverent and profane," Mikah said through his clenched teeth, as he went to the controls. "You attempt to kill us both. You have no respect for your own life or

18

mine. You are a man who deserves the worst punishment the law allows."

"I'm a gambler," Jason laughed, "not at all as bad as you say. I take chances—but I only take them when the odds are right. You were carrying me back to certain death. The worst my wrecking the controls can do is to administer the same fate. So I took a chance. There is a bigger risk factor for you, of course, but I'm afraid I didn't take that into consideration. After all, this entire affair is your idea. You'll just have to take the consequences of your own actions, and not scold me for them."

"You are perfectly right," Mikah said quietly. "I should have been more alert. Now will you tell me what to do to save *both* our lives. None of the controls work."

"None! Did you try the emergency override? The big red switch under the safety housing."

"I did. It is dead too."

Jason slumped back into the seat. It was a moment before he could speak. "Read one of your books, Mikah," he said at last. "Seek consolation in your philosophy. There's nothing we can do. It's all up to the computer now, and whatever is left of the circuits."

"Can we help—can we repair anything?"

"Are you a ship technician? I'm not. We would probably do more harm than good."

It took two ship-days of very erratic flight to reach the planet. A haze of clouds obscured the atmosphere. They approached from the night side, and no details were visible. Or lights.

"If there were cities we would see their lights—wouldn't we?" Mikah asked.

"Not necessarily. Could be storms. Could be enclosed cities. Could be only ocean in this hemisphere."

"Or it could be that there are no people down there," Mikah said. "Even if the ship should get us down safely, what will it matter? We will be trapped for the rest of our lives on this lost planet, at the end of the universe."

"Don't be so cheerful," Jason said. "How about taking off these cuffs while we go down? It will probably be a rough landing and I'd like to have some kind of a chance."

Mikah frowned at him. "Will you give me your word of honor that you will not try to escape during the landing?"

"No. And if I gave it—would you believe it? If you let me loose, you take your chances. Let's neither of us think it will be any different."

"I have my duty to do," Mikah said. Jason remained locked in the chair.

They were in the atmosphere, and the gentle sighing against the hull quickly climbed the scale to a shrill scream. The drive cut out and they were in free fall. Air friction heated the outer hull white-hot, and the interior temperature quickly rose in spite of the cooling unit.

"What is happening?" Mikah asked. "You are more acquainted with these matters. Are we through—are we going to crash?"

"Maybe. It can only be one of two things. Either the whole works have folded up—in which case we are going to be scattered in very small pieces all over the landscape; or the computer is saving itself for one last effort. I hope that's it. They build computers smart these days, all sorts of problem-solving circuits. The hull and engines are in good shape —but the controls are spotty and unreliable. In a case like this, a good human pilot would let the ship drop as far and fast as it could before switching on the drive. Then he'd turn it on full—thirteen G's or more, whatever he figured the passengers could take on the couches. The hull would take a beating, but who cares? The control circuits would be used the shortest amount of time in the simplest manner."

"Do you think that is happening now?" Mikah asked, getting into his acceleration chair.

"That's what I *hope* is happening. Are you going to unlock the cuffs before you go to bed? It could be a bad landing, and we might want to go places in a hurry."

Mikah considered, then took out his gun. "I will unlock you, but I intend to shoot if you try anything. Once we are down, you will be locked in again."

"Thanks for small blessings," Jason said when he was free, rubbing his wrists.

Deceleration jumped on them, kicked the air from their lungs in uncontrollable gasps, sank them deep into the yielding couches. Mikah's gun was pressed into his chest, too heavy to lift. It made no difference—Jason could not stand nor move. He hovered on the border of consciousness, his vision flickering behind a black and red haze.

Just as suddenly the pressure was gone.

They were still falling.

The drive groaned in the stern of the ship, and relays chattered. But it didn't start again. The two men stared at each other, unmoving, for the unmeasurable unit of time that the ship fell.

As the ship dropped it turned, and it hit at an angle. The end came for Jason in an engulfing wave of thunder, shock, and pain. The sudden impact pushed him against the restraining straps, burst them with the inertia of his body, hurled him across the control room. His last conscious thought was to protect his head. He was lifting his arms when he struck the wall.

There is a cold that is so chilling it is a pain, not a temperature. A cold that slices into the flesh before it numbs and kills.

Jason came to with the sound of his own voice crying hoarsely. The cold was so great it filled the universe. It was cold water, he realized as he coughed it from his mouth and nose. Something was around him, and it took an effort to recognize it as Mikah's arm; he was holding Jason's face above the surface while he swam. A receding blackness in the water could only have been the ship, giving off bubbles and groans as it died. The cold water didn't hurt now, and Jason was just relaxing when he felt something solid under his feet.

"Stand up and walk, curse you," Mikah gasped hoarsely. "I can't . . . carry you . . . can't carry myself. . . ."

They floundered out of the water side by side, four-legged crawling beasts that could not stand erect. Everything had an unreality about it, and Jason found it hard to think. He should not stop, that he was sure of, but what else could he do?

There was a flickering in the darkness, a wavering light coming towards them. Jason could not speak, but he heard Mikah cry out for help. The light came nearer; it was some kind of flare or torch, held high. Mikah pulled to his feet as the flame approached.

It was like a nightmare. It wasn't a man but a thing that held the flare. A thing of sharp angles, fang-faced and horrible. It had a clubbed extremity with which it struck down Mikah, who fell wordlessly, and the creature turned towards Jason. He had no strength to fight with, though he struggled to get to his feet. His fingers scratched at the frosted sand, but he could not rise; and exhausted with this last effort, he fell face down.

Unconsciousness pulled at his brain, but he would not submit. The flickering torchlight came closer, and the scuffle of heavy feet in the sand. He could not have this horror behind him, and with the last of his strength he levered himself over and lay on his back, staring up at the thing that stood over him, with the darkness of exhaustion filming his eyes.

CHAPTER FOUR

It did not kill him at once, but stood staring down at him; and as the slow seconds ticked by and Jason was still alive, he forced himself to consider this menace that had appeared from the blackness.

"*K'e vi stas el . . . ?*" the creature said, and for the first time Jason realized it was human. The meaning of the question picked at the edge of his exhausted brain; he felt he could almost understand it, though he had never heard the language before. He tried to answer, but there was only a hoarse gurgle from his throat.

"*Ven k'n torcoy—r'pidu!*"

More lights sprang from the darkness inland, and with them the sound of running feet. As they came closer, Jason had a clearer look at the man above him and could understand why he had mistaken him for some non-human creature. His limbs were completely wrapped in lengths of stained leather, his chest and body protected by thick overlapping leather plates covered with blood-red designs. Over his head was fitted the cochleate-shell of some animal, spiraling to a point in front; two small openings had been drilled in it for eye holes. Great, finger-long teeth had been set in the lower edge of the shell to heighten the already fearsome appearance. The only thing at all human about the creature was the matted and filthy beard that trickled out of the shell below the teeth. There were too many other details for Jason to absorb quickly; something bulky was slung behind one shoulder, dark objects at the waist; a heavy club reached and prodded Jason in the ribs, and he was too close to unconsciousness to resist.

A guttural command halted the torchbearers a full five meters from the spot where Jason lay. He wondered vaguely why the armored man had not let them approach closer, since the light from their torches barely reached this far; everything on this planet seemed inexplicable.

For a few moments Jason must have lost consciousness, for when he looked again the torch was stuck in the sand at his side and the armored man had one of Jason's boots off and was pulling at the other. Jason could only writhe feebly but could not prevent the theft; for some reason he could not force his body to follow his will. His sense of time seemed to have altered as well, and though every second dragged heavily by, events occurred with startling rapidity. The boots were gone now and the man fumbled at Jason's clothes, stopping every few seconds to glance up at the row of torchbearers.

The magnetic seals were alien to the strange creature, the sharp teeth sewn onto the leather over his knuckles dug into Jason's flesh as he struggled to open the seals or to tear the resistant metalcloth. He was growling with impatience when he accidentally touched the release button on the medikit and it dropped into his hand. This shining gadget seemed to please him; but when one of the sharp needles slipped through his thick handcoverings and stabbed him he howled with rage throwing the machine down, and grinding it into a splintered ruin in the sand. The loss of his irreplaceable device goaded Jason into motion : he sat up and was trying to reach the medikit when unconsciousness surged over him.

Sometime before dawn the pain in his head drove him reluctantly back to awareness. There were some foul-smelling hides draped over him that retained a little of his body heat. He pulled away the stifling fold that covered his face and stared up at the stars, cold points of light that glittered in the frigid night. The air was a stimulant, and he sucked in deep gasps of it that burned his throat but seemed to clear his thoughts. For the first time he realized that his disorientation had been caused by that crack on the head he had received when the ship crashed; his exploring fingers found a swollen rawness on his skull. He must have a brain concussion : that would explain his earlier inability to move or think straight. The cold air was numbing his face, and he willingly pulled the hairy skin back over his head.

He wondered what had happened to Mikah Samon after the local thug in the horror outfit had bashed him with the club. This was a messy and unexpected end for the man after he had managed to survive the crash of the ship. Jason had no special affection for the undernourished zealot, but he did owe him a life. Mikah had saved him after the crash, only to be murdered himself by this assassin.

Jason made a mental note to kill the man just as soon as he was physically up to it; at the same time he was a little

24

astonished at his reflexive acceptance of the need for this bloodthirsty atonement of a life for a life. Apparently his long stay on Pyrrus had trodden down his normal dislike for killing except in self-defense, and from what he had seen so far of this world the Pyrran training would certainly be most useful. The sky showed grey through a tear in the hide and he pushed the covering back to look at the dawn.

Mikah Samon lay next to him, his head projecting from a covering fur. His hair was matted and caked with dark blood, but he was still breathing.

"Harder to kill than I thought," Jason muttered as he levered himself painfully up onto one elbow and took a good look at this world where his spaceship sabotage had landed him.

It was a grim desert, lumped with huddled bodies, like the aftermath of a battle at world's end. A few of them were stumbling to their feet, holding their skins around them, the only signs of life in that immense waste of gritty sand. On one side a ridge of dunes cut off sight of the sea, but he could hear the dull boom of waves on the shore. White frost rimed the ground and the chill wind made his eyes blink and water. On the top of the dunes a remembered figure suddenly appeared, the armored man, doing something with what appeared to be lengths of rope; there was a metallic tinkling, suddenly cut off. Mikah Samon groaned and stirred.

"How do you feel?" Jason asked. "Those are two of the finest blood-shot eyes I have ever seen."

"Where am I . . . ?"

"Now, that is a bright and original question—I didn't pick you for the type who watched historical space opera on the TV. I have no idea where we are—but I can give you a brief synopsis of how we arrived here, if you are up to it."

"I remember we swam ashore, then something evil came from the darkness, like a demon from hell. We fought . . ."

"And he bashed in your head—one quick blow, and that was about all the fight there was. I had a better look at your demon, though I was in no better condition to fight him than you were. He's a man dressed in a weird outfit out of an addict's nightmare, and he appears to be the boss of this crew of rugged campers. Other than that, I have little idea of what is going on—except that he stole my boots, and

I'm going to get them back if I have to kill him for them."

"Do not lust after material things," Mikah intoned seriously. "And do not talk of killing a man for material gain. You are evil, Jason, and . . . My boots are gone—and my clothes too!"

Mikah had thrown back his covering skins and made this startling discovery. "Belial!" he roared. "Asmodeus, Abaddon, Apollyon, and Baal-zebub!"

"Very nice," Jason said admiringly. "You really have been studying up on your demonology. Were you just listing them—or calling on them for aid?"

"Silence, blasphemer! I have been robbed!" He rose to his feet, and the wind whistling around his almost bare body quickly gave his skin a faint touch of blue. "I am going to find the evil creature that did this and force him to return what is mine."

Mikah turned to leave, but Jason reached out and grabbed his ankle with a wrestling grip, twisted it, and brought the man thudding to the ground. The fall dazed him, and Jason pulled the skins back over the rawboned form.

"We're even," Jason said. "You saved my life last night; just now I saved your. You're bare-handed and wounded—while the old man of the mountain up there is a walking armory, and anyone with the personality to wear that kind of an outfit will kill you as easily as he picks his teeth. So take it easy and try to avoid trouble. There's a way out of this mess—there's a way out of *every* mess if you look for it —and I'm going to find it. In fact, I'm going to take a walk right now and start my research. Agreed?"

A groan was the only answer, for Mikah was unconscious again, fresh blood seeping from his injured scalp. Jason stood up and wrapped the hides about his body as some protection from the wind, tying the loose ends together. Then he kicked through the sand until he found a smooth rock that would fit inside his fist with just the end protruding, and thus armed he made his way through the stirring forms of the sleepers.

When he returned, Mikah was conscious again, and the sun was well above the horizon. The people were all awake now, a shuffling, scratching herd of about thirty men, women, and children. They were identical in their filth and crude skin wrappings, milling about with random movements, or sitting blankly on the ground. They showed no interest at all in the two strangers. Jason handed a tarred leather cup to Mikah and squatted next to him.

"Drink that. It's water, the only thing there seems to be here to drink. I didn't find any food." He still had the stone in his hand, and while he talked he rubbed it on the sand : the end was moist and red and some long hairs were stuck in it.

"I took a good look around this camp, and there's very little more than you can see from here. Just this crowd of broken-down types, with few bundles rolled in hide, and some of them are carrying skin water bottles. They have a simple me-stronger pecking order, so I pecked a bit and we can drink. Food comes next."

"Who are they? What are they doing?" Mikah asked, mumbling a little, obviously still suffering the aftereffects of the blow. Jason looked at the contused skull, and decided not to touch it. The wound had bled freely and the blood had now clotted. Washing it off with the highly dubious water would accomplish little, and might add infection to their other troubles.

"I'm only sure of one thing," Jason said. "They're slaves. I don't know why they are here, what they are doing, or where they are going, but their status is painfully clear— ours too. Old Nasty up there on the hill is the boss. The rest of us are slaves."

"Slaves!" Mikah excaimed, horrified, the word penetrating through the pain in his head. "It is abominable. The slaves must be freed."

"No lectures, please, and try to be realistic—even if it hurts. There are only two slaves that need freeing here, you and I. These people seem nicely adjusted to the *status quo*, and I see no reason to change it. I'm not starting any abolitionist campaigns until I can see my way clearly out of this mess, and I probably won't start any then either. This planet has been going on a long time without me, and will probably keep rolling along once I'm gone."

"Coward! You must fight for the Truth, and the Truth will make you free."

"I can hear those capital letters again," Jason groaned. "The only thing right now that is going to make me free is me. Which may be bad poetry, but it is still the truth. The situation here is rough but not unbeatable, so listen and learn. The boss—his name is Ch'aka—seems to have gone

27

off on a hunt of some kind. He's not far away and will be back soon, so I'll try to give you the entire setup quickly. I thought I recognized the language, and I was right. It's a corrupt form of Esperanto, the language all the Terido worlds speak. This altered language, plus the fact that these people live about one step above the Stone Age culture, is pretty sure evidence that they are cut off from any contact with the rest of the galaxy, though I hope not. There may be a trading base somewhere on the planet, and if there is we'll find it later. We have enough other things to worry about right now, but at least we can speak the language. These people have contracted a lot of sounds and lost some, and they've even introduced a glottal stop—something that *no* language needs; but with a little effort the meaning can still be made out."

"I do not speak Esperanto."

"Then learn it. It's easy enough, even in this jumbled form. Now keep still and listen. These creatures are born and bred slaves, and it is all they know. There is a little squabbling in the ranks, with the bigger ones pushing the work on the weak ones when Ch'aka isn't looking, but I have that situation well in hand. Ch'aka is our big problem, and we have to find out a lot more things before we can tackle him. He is boss, fighter, father, provider, and destiny for this mob, and he seems to know his job. So try to be a good slave for a while."

"Slave! I!" Mikah arched his back and tried to rise. Jason pushed him back to the ground—harder than was necessary.

"Yes, you—and me too. That is the only way we are going to survive in this arrangement. Do what everyone else does; obey orders, and you stand a good chance of staying alive until we can find a way out of this tangle."

Mikah's answer was drowned out in a roar from the dunes as Ch'aka returned. The slaves climbed quickly to their feet, grabbing up their bundles, and began to form a single wide-spaced line. Jason helped Mikah to stand and wrap strips of skin around his feet, then supported most of his weight as they stumbled to a place in the open formation. Once they were all in position, Ch'aka kicked the nearest one and they began walking slowly forward, looking carefully at the ground as they went. Jason had no idea of the significance of this action, but as long as he and Mikah weren't bothered it didn't matter : he had enough work cut out for him just to keep the wounded man on his feet. Somehow Mikah managed to dredge up enough strength to keep going.

One of the slaves pointed down and shouted, and the line stopped. He was too far away for Jason to make out the cause of the excitement, but the man bent over and scratched a hole with a short length of pointed wood. In a few seconds he dug up something round and not quite as big as his hand. He raised it over his head and brought the thing to Ch'aka at a shambling run. The slave-master took it and bit off a chunk, and when the man who had found it turned away he gave him a lusty kick. The line moved forward again.

Two more of the mysterious objects were found, both of which Ch'aka ate. Only when his immediate hunger was satisfied did he make any attempt to be the good provider. When the next one was found he called over a slave and threw the object into a crudely woven basket the slave was carrying on his back. After this the basket-toting slave walked directly in front of Ch'aka, who was carefully watchful that every one of the things that was dug up went into the basket. Jason wondered what they were—and they were edible, an angry rumbling in his stomach reminded him.

The slave next in line to Jason shouted and pointed to the sand. Jason let Mikah sink to a sitting position when they stopped, and watched with interest as the slave attacked the ground with his piece of wood, scratching around a tiny sprig of green that projected from the desert sand. His burrowings uncovered a wrinkled grey object, a root or tuber of some kind, from which the green leaves were growing. It appeared to Jason as edible as a piece of stone, but obviously not to the slave, who drooled heavily and actually had the temerity to sniff the root. Ch'aka howled with anger at this, and when the slave had dropped the root into the basket with the others he received a kick so strong that he had to limp back painfully to his position in the line.

Soon after this Ch'aka called a halt, and the tattered slaves huddled around while he poked through the basket. He called them over one at a time and gave them one or more of the roots, according to some merit system of his own. The basket was almost empty when he poked his club at Jason.

"*K'e nam h'vas vi?*" he asked.

"*Mia namo estas Jason, mia amiko estas Mikah.*"

Jason had answered in correct Esperanto, which Ch'aka seemed to understand well enough, for he grunted and dug through the contents of the basket. His masked face stared at them, and Jason could feel the impact of the unseen watching eyes. The club pointed again.

"Where you come from? That your ship that burn, sink?"

"That was our ship. We come from far away."

"From other side of ocean?" This was apparently the largest distance the slaver could imagine.

"From the other side of the ocean, correct." Jason was in no mood to deliver a lecture on astronomy. "When do we eat?"

"You a rich man in your country, got a ship, got shoes. Now I got your shoes. You a slave here. My slave. You both my slaves."

"I'm your slave, I'm your slave," Jason said resignedly. "But even slaves have to eat. Where's the food?"

Ch'aka grubbed around in the basket until he found a tiny withered root that he broke in half and threw onto the sand in front of Jason.

"Work hard, you get more."

Jason picked up the pieces, and brushed away as much of the dirt as he could. He handed one piece to Mikah and took a tentative bite out of the other one: it was gritty with sand and tasted like slightly rancid wax. It took a distinct effort to eat the repulsive thing, but he did. Without a doubt it was food, no matter how unwholesome, and would do until something better came along.

"What did you talk about?" Mikah asked, grinding his own portion between his teeth.

"Just swapping lies. He thinks we're his slaves, and I agreed. But it's just temporary," Jason added as anger colored Mikah's face and he started to climb to his feet. Jason pulled him back down. "This is a strange planet; you're injured, we have no food or water, and no idea at all how to survive in this place. The only thing we can do to stay alive is to go along with what Old Ugly there says. If he wants to call us slaves, fine—we're slaves."

"Better to die free than to live in chains!"

"Will you stop the nonsense! Better to live in chains and learn how to get rid of them. That way you end up alive-free rather than dead-free, a much more attractive state. Now shut up and eat. We can't do anything until you are out of the walking-wounded class."

For the rest of the day the line of walkers plodded across the sand, and in addition to helping Mikah, Jason found two of the *krenoj*, the edible roots. They stopped before dusk and dropped gratefully to the sand. When the food was divided they received a slightly larger portion, as evidence perhaps of Jason's attention to the work. Both men were exhausted and fell asleep as soon as it was dark.

During the following morning they had their first break from the walking routine. Their food-searching always paralleled the unseen sea, and one slave walked the crest of the dunes that hid the water from sight. He must have seen something of interest, for he leaped down from the mound and waved both hands wildly. Ch'aka ran heavily to the dunes and talked with the scout, then booted the man from his presence.

Jason watched with growing interest as he unwrapped the bulky package slung from his back and disclosed an efficient-looking crossbow, cocking it by winding on a built-in crank. This complicated and deadly piece of machinery seemed very much out of place with the primitive slave-holding society, and Jason wished that he could get a better look at the device. Ch'aka fumbled a quarrel from another pouch and fitted it to the bow.

The slaves sat silently on the sand while their master stalked along the base of the dunes, then wormed his way over them and out of sight, creeping silently on his stomach. A few minutes later there was a scream of pain from behind the dunes and all the slaves jumped to their feet and raced to see. Jason left Mikah where he lay and was in the first rank of observers that broke over the hillocks and onto the shore.

They stopped at the usual distance and shouted compliments about the quality of the shot and what a mighty hunter Ch'aka was. Jason had to admit there was a certain truth in the claims. A large, furred amphibian lay at the water's edge, the fletched end of the crossbow bolt projecting from its thick neck and a thin stream of blood running down to mix with the surging waves.

"Meat ! Meat ! today !"

"Ch'aka kills the *rosmaro* ! Ch'aka is wonderful !"

31

"Hail, Ch'aka, great provider!" Jason shouted to get into he swing of things. "When do we eat?"

The master ignored the slaves, sitting heavily on the dune until he regained his breath after the stalk. Then, after cocking the crossbow again, he went over to the beast and with his knife cut out the quarrel, notching it against the bowstring still dripping with blood.

"Get wood for fire," he commanded. "You, Opisweni, you use the knife."

Shuffling backwards, Ch'aka sat down on a hillock and pointed the crossbow at the slave who approached the kill. Ch'aka had left his knife in the animal and Opisweni pulled it free and began methodically to flay and butcher the beast. All the time he worked he carefully kept his back turned to Ch'aka and the aimed bow.

"A trusting soul, our slave driver," Jason said to himself as he joined the others in searching the shore for driftwood. Ch'aka had the weapons, but he had a constant fear of assassination as well. If Opisweni tried to use the knife for anything other than the intended piece of work, he would get the crossbow quarrel in the back of the head. Very efficient.

Enough driftwood was found to make a sizeable fire, and when Jason returned with his contribution the *rosmaro* had been hacked into large chunks. Ch'aka kicked his slaves away from the heap of wood and produced a small device from another of his sacks. Interested, Jason pushed as close as he dared, into the front rank of the watching circle. Though he had never seen a firemaker before, the operation of it was obvious to him. A spring-loaded arm drove a fragment of stone against a piece of steel, sparks flew out and were caught in a cup of tinder, where Ch'aka blew on them until they burst into flame.

Where had the firemaker and the crossbow come from? They were evidence of a higher level of culture than that possessed by those slave-holding nomads. This was the first bit of evidence Jason had seen that there might be more to the cultural life of this planet than they had seen since their landing. Later, while the others were gorging themselves on the seared meat, he drew Mikah aside and pointed this out.

"There's hope yet. These illiterate thugs never manufactured that crossbow or firemaker. We must find out where they came from, and see about getting there ourselves. I had a look at the quarrel when Ch'aka pulled it out, and I'll swear that it was turned from a piece of steel."

"This has significance?" Mikah asked, puzzled.

"It means an industrial society, and possible interstellar contact."

"Then we must ask Ch'aka where he obtained them and leave at once. There will be authorities, we will contact them, explain the situation, obtain transportation to Cassylia. I will not place you under arrest again until that time."

"How considerate of you!" Jason said, lifting one eyebrow. Mikah was absolutely impossible, and Jason probed at his moral armor to see if there were any weak spots. "Won't you feel guilty about bringing me back to get killed? After all, we are companions in trouble—and I did save your life."

"I will grieve, Jason. I can see that though you are evil you are not completely evil, and given the right training could be fitted for a useful place in society. But my personal grief must not be allowed to alter events : you forget that you committed a crime and must pay the penalty."

Ch'aka belched cavernously inside his shell helmet and howled at his slaves.

"Enough eating, you pigs! You get fat. Wrap the meat and carry it—we have light yet to look for *krenoj*. Move!"

Once more the line was formed and began its slow pace across the desert. More of the edible roots were found, and once they stopped briefly to fill the waterbags at a spring that bubbled up out of the sand. The sun dropped towards the horizon, and what little warmth it possessed was absorbed by a bank of clouds. Jason looked around and shivered; then he noticed the line of dots moving on the horizon. He nudged Mikah, who still leaned heavily on him.

"Looks like company coming. I wonder where they fit into the program."

Pain had blurred Mikah's attention and he took no notice and, surprisingly enough, neither did any of the other slaves, nor Ch'aka. The dots expanded and became another row of marchers, apparently absorbed in the same task as Ch'aka's group. They plodded forward, making a slow examination of the sand, and were followed behind by the solitary figure of their master. The two lines slowly approached each other, paralleling the shore.

Near the dunes was a crude mound of stones and Ch'aka's

33

line of slaves stopped as soon as they reached it, dropping with satisfied grunts onto the sand. The cairn was obviously a border marker, and Ch'aka went to it and rested his foot on one of the stones, watching while the other line of slaves approached. They too stopped at the cairn and settled to the ground : both groups stared with dull-eyed lack of interest, and only the slave-masters showed any animation. The other master stopped a good ten paces before he reached Ch'aka and waved an evil-looking stone hammer over his head.

"Hate you, Ch'aka !" he roared.

"Hate you, Fasimba !" boomed back the answer.

The exchange was as formal as a *pas de deux*, and just about as warlike. Both men shook their weapons and shouted a few insults, then settled down to a quiet conversation. Fasimba was garbed in the same type of hideous and fear-inspiring outfit as Ch'aka, differing only in details. Instead of a conch, Fasimba's head was encased in the skull of one of the amphibious *rosmaroj*, brightened up with some extra tusks and horns. The differences between the two men were all minor, and mostly a matter of decoration or variation of weapon design. They were obviously slave-masters and equals.

"Killed a *rosmaro* today, second time in ten days," Ch'aka said.

"You got a good piece coast. Plenty *rosmaroj*. Where the two slaves you owe me ?"

"I owe you two slaves ?"

"You owe me two slaves. Don't play like stupid. I got the iron arrows for you from the *d'zertanoj*. One slave you paid with died. You still owe other one."

"I got two slaves for you. I got two slaves I pulled out of the ocean."

"You got a good piece coast."

Ch'aka walked down his line of slaves until he came to the overbold one he had half crippled with a kick the day before. Pulling him to his feet, he booted him towards the other group.

"Here a good one," he said, delivering the goods with a parting kick.

"Looks skinny. Not too good."

"No, all muscles. Works hard. Doesn't eat much."

"You're a liar !"

"Hate you, Fasimba !"

"Hate you, Ch'aka! Where's the other one?"

"Got a good one. Stranger from the ocean. He can tell you funny stories, work hard."

Jason turned in time to avoid the full force of the kick, but it was still strong enough to knock him sprawling. Before he could get up, Ch'aka had clutched Mikah Samon by the arm and dragged him across the invisible line to the other group of slaves. Fasimba stalked over to examine him, prodding him with a spiked toe.

"Don't look good. Big hole on the head."

"He works hard," Ch'aka said. "Hole almost healed. He very strong."

"You give me new one if he dies?" Fasimba asked doubtfully.

"I'll give you. Hate you, Fasimba!"

"Hate *you*, Ch'aka!"

The slaves herds were prodded to their feet and moved back the way they had come.

Jason shouted to Ch'aka. "Wait! Don't sell my friend. We work better together. You can get rid of someone else. . ."

The slaves gaped at this sudden outburst and Ch'aka wheeled, raising his club.

"You shut up. You're a slave. You tell me once more to do what and I kill you."

Jason kept still, since it was obvious that this was the only thing he could do. He had a few qualms about Mikah's possible fate: if he survived the wound, he was certainly not the type to bow to the inevitabilities of slave-holding life. But Jason had done his best to save him, and that was that. Now Jason would think about Jason for a while.

They made a brief march before dark, just until the other slaves were out of sight; then they stopped for the night. Jason settled himself into the lee of a mound that broke the force of the wind a bit and unwrapped a piece of scorched meat he had salvaged from the earlier feast. It was tough and oily, but far superior to the barely edible *krenoj* that made up the greater part of the native diet. He chewed noisily on the bone and watched while one of the other slaves sidled over towards him.

"Give me some of your meat?" the slave asked in a whining voice, and only when she had spoken did Jason realize that this was a girl; all the slaves looked alike in their matted hair and skin wrappings. He ripped off a chunk of meat.

"Here. Sit down and eat it. What's your name?" In exchange for his generosity, he intended to get some information from the girl.

"Ijale." Still standing, she tore at the meat, held tightly in one fist while the index finger of her free hand scratched in her tangled hair.

"Where do you come from? Did you always live here—like this?" How do you ask a slave if she has always been a slave?

"Not here. I come from Bul'wajo first, then Fasimba, now I belong to Ch'aka."

"What or who is Bul'wajo? Someone like our boss Ch'aka?"

She nodded, gnawing at the meat.

"And the *d'zertanoj* that Fasimba gets his arrows from—who are they?"

"You don't know much," she said, finishing the meat and licking the grease from her fingers.

"I know enough to have meat when you don't have any—so don't abuse my hospitality. Who are the *d'zertanoj*?"

"Everyone knows who they are." She shrugged with incomprehension and looked for a soft spot in the sand to sit down. "They live in the desert. They go around in *caroj*. They stink. They have many nice things. One of them gave me my best thing. If I show it to you, you won't take it?"

"No, I won't touch it. But I would like to see anything they have made. Here, here's some more meat. Now let me see your best thing."

Ijale rooted in her skins for a hidden pocket and dragged out something concealed in her clenched fist. She held out her hand proudly and opened it, and there was enough light left for Jason to make out the rough form of a red glass bead.

"Isn't this very nice?" she asked.

"Very nice," Jason agreed, and for an instant felt a touch of real compassion when he looked at the pathetic bauble. This girl's ancestors had come to this planet in spaceships, with a knowledge of the most advanced sciences. Cut off, their children had degenerated into this: barely conscious slaves, who could prize a worthless piece of glass above all things.

"All right now," Ijale said, settling into the sand on her back. She unwrapped some skins and began to pull the others up around her waist.

"Relax," Jason told her. "The meat was a present—you don't have to pay for it."

"You don't want me?" she asked, surprised pulling the skins back over her bare legs. "You do not like me? You think I am too ugly?'

"You're lovely," Jason lied. "Let's just say that I'm too tired."

Was the girl ugly or lovely? He couldn't tell. Her unwashed and tangled hair covered half of her face, while dirt threw an obscuring film over the rest. Her lips were chapped raw, and a red bruise covered one cheek.

"Let me stay with you tonight, even if you are too old to want me. Mzil'kazi wants me all the time, and he hurts me. See, there he is now."

The man she pointed to was watching from a healthy distance and skittered back even further when Jason looked up.

"Don't worry about Mzil'," Jason said. "We settled our relationship the first day I was here. You may have noticed the bump on his head." He reached for a rock and the watcher ran swiftly away.

"I like you. I'll show you my best thing again."

"I like you too. No, not now. Too many good things too fast will only spoil me. Good night."

CHAPTER FIVE

Ijale stayed near Jason the next day, and took the next station in line when the endless *krenoj* hunt began. Whenever it was possible he questioned her, and before noon had extracted all of her meager knowledge of affairs beyond the barren coastal plain where they lived. The ocean was a mystery that produced edible animals, fish, and an occasional human corpse. Ships could be seen from time to time offshore, but nothing was known about them. On the other side the territory was bounded by desert even more inhospitable than the one in which they scratched out their existence—a waste of lifeless sand, habitable only by the *d'zertanoj* and their mysterious *caroj*. These last might be animals—or perhaps mechanical transportation of some kind; either was possible from Ijale's vague description. Ocean, coast, and desert—these made up all of her world, and she could conceive nothing that might exist beyond.

Jason knew there was more; the crossbow was proof enough of that, and he had every intention of finding out where it came from. In order to do that he was going to have to change his slave status when the proper time came. He was developing a certain facility in dodging Ch'aka's heavy boot; the work was never hard, and there was ample food. Being a slave left him with no responsibilities other than obeying orders, and he had ample opportunity to discover what he could about this planet, so that when he finally did leave he would be as well prepared as was possible.

Later in the day another column of marching slaves was sighted in the distance, on a course paralleling their own, and Jason expected a repeat performance of the previous day's meeting. He was agreeably surprised that it was not. The sight of the others threw Ch'aka into an immediate rage that sent his slaves rushing for safety in all directions. By leaping into the air, howling with anger, and beating his club against his thick leather armor, he manged to work himself into quite a state before starting off on a slogging run. Jason followed close behind him, greatly interested by this new turn of affairs.

Ahead of them the other group of slaves scattered, and

from their midst burst another armed and armored figure. The two leaders churned towards each other at top speed, and Jason hoped for a shattering crash when they met. However, they slowed before they hit and began circling each other, spitting curses.

"Hate you, M'shika!"

"Hate you, Ch'aka!"

The words were the same, but they were shouted with fierce meaning, with no touch of formality this time.

"Kill you, M'shika! You coming again on my part of the ground with your carrion-meat slaves!"

"You lie, Ch'aka—this ground mine from way back."

"I kill you way back!"

Ch'aka leaped in as he screamed the words and swung a blow with his club that would have broken the other man in two if it had connected. But M'shika was expecting this and fell back, swinging a counterblow with his own club, which Ch'aka easily avoided. There followed a quick exchange of clubwork that did little more than fan the air, until suddenly both men were locked together and the fight began in earnest.

They rolled together on the ground, grunting savagely, tearing at each other. The heavy clubs were of no use this close and were dropped in favor of knives and knees: Jason could understand now why Ch'aka had the long tusks strapped to his kneecaps. It was a no-holds-barred fight, and each man was trying as hard as possible to kill his opponent. The leather armor made this difficult and the struggle continued, littering the sand with broken-off animal teeth, discarded weapons, and other debris. It looked as if it would be a draw, when both men separated for a breather; but they dived right back in again.

It was Ch'aka who broke the stalemate when he plunged his dagger into the ground and on the next roll caught the handle in his mouth. Holding his opponent's arms in both his hands he plunged his head down and managed to find a weak spot in the other's armor. M'shika howled and pulled free, and when he climbed to his feet blood was running down his arm and dripping from his fingertips. Ch'aka jumped after him but the wounded man grabbed up his club in time to ward off the charge.

Stumbling backwards, he managed to pick up most of his discarded weapons with his wounded arm and beat a hasty retreat. Ch'aka ran after him a short way, shouting praise of his own strength and abilities and of his opponent's cowardice. Jason saw a short horn from some sea animal lying in the churned-up sand and quickly picked it up before Ch'aka turned back.

Once his enemy had been chased out of sight, Ch'aka carefully searched the battle ground and salvaged anything of military value. Though there were still some hours of daylight left, he signaled that this was a halt and distributed the evening ration of *krenoj*.

Jason sat and chewed his portion reflectively, while Ijale leaned against his side, her shoulder moving rhythmically as she scratched some hidden mite. Lice were inescapable; they hid in the crevices of the badly cured hides and emerged to the warmth of human flesh. Jason had his quota of the pests, and found his scratching keeping time with hers. This syncopation of scratching triggered the anger that had been building within him, slow and unnoticed.

"I'm serving notice," he said, jumping to his feet. "I'm through with this slave business. Which way is the nearest spot in the desert where I can find the *d'zertanoj*?"

"Over there, a two-day walk. How are you going to kill Ch'aka?"

"I'm not going to kill Ch'aka, I'm just leaving. I've enjoyed his hospitality and his boot long enough."

"You can't do that," she gasped. "You will be killed."

"Ch'aka can't very well kill me if I'm not here."

"Everybody will kill you. That is the law. Runaway slaves are always killed."

Jason sat down again and cracked another chunk from his *kreno* and ruminated over it. "You've talked me into staying a while. But I have no particular desire now to kill Ch'aka, even though he did steal my boots. And I don't see how killing him will help me any."

"You are stupid. After you kill Ch'aka you'll be the new Ch'aka. Then you can do what you want."

Of course. Now that he had been told, the social setup appeared obvious. Because he had seen slaves and slaveholders, Jason had held the mistaken notion that they were different classes of society, when in reality there was only one class, what might be called the dog-eat-dog class. He should have been aware of this when he had seen how careful Ch'aka was never to allow anyone within striking distance of him, and how he vanished each night to some hidden spot. This was free enterprise with a vengeance, carried to its absolute extreme, with every man out for himself, every other man's hand turned against him, and your station in life determined by the strength of your arm and the speed of your reflexes. Anyone who stayed alone placed himself outside this society and was therefore an enemy of it and sure to be killed on sight. All of which added up to the fact that he had to kill Ch'aka if he wanted to get ahead. He still had no desire to do it; nevertheless he had to.

That night Jason watched Ch'aka when he slipped away from the others, and made a careful note of the direction that he took. Of course the slave-master would circle about before he concealed himself, but with a little luck Jason would find him. And kill him. He had no special love of midnight assassinations, and until landing on this planet he had always believed that killing a sleeping man was a cowardly way to terminate another's existence. But special conditions demand special solutions, and he was no match for the heavily armored man in open combat; therefore the assassin's knife—or rather, the sharpened horn.

He managed to doze fitfully until some time after midnight; then he slipped silently from under his skin coverings. Ijale knew he was leaving; he could see her open eyes in the starlight, but she did not move nor say a word. Silently he skirted the sleepers and crept into the darkness between the dunes.

Finding Ch'aka in the wilderness of the desert night was not easy, but Jason persisted. He made careful sweeps in wider and wider arcs, working his way out from the sleeping slaves. There were gullies and shadowed ravines, and all of them had to be searched with utmost care. The slave-master must be sleeping in one of them and would be alert for any sound.

The fact that Ch'aka had taken special precautions to guard against assassination was apparent to Jason only after he heard the bell ring. It was a tiny sound, barely detectable, but he froze instantly. There was a thin strand pressing against his arm, and when he drew back carefully the bell sounded again. He cursed silently for his stupidity, remembering only now about the bells he had heard before from Ch'aka's sleeping site. The slaver must surround himself every night with a network of string that would sound alarm bells if anyone attempted to approach in the dark. Slowly and soundlessly Jason drew back deeper into the gulley.

With a thud of rushing feet Ch'aka appeared, swinging his club around his head and coming directly towards Jason. Jason rolled desperately sideways and the club crashed into the ground, then he was up and running at top speed down the gulley. Rocks twisted under his feet and he knew that if he tripped he was dead, but he had no choice other than flight. The heavily armored Ch'aka could not keep up with him, and Jason managed to stay on his feet until the other was left behind. Ch'aka shouted with rage and hurled curses after him, but he could not catch him. Jason, panting for breath, vanished into the darkness.

He made a slow circle back towards the sleeping camp. He knew the noise would have roused them and he stayed away for an estimated hour, shivering in the icy predawn, before he slipped back to his waiting skins. The sky was beginning to grey and he lay awake wondering if he had been recognized : he didn't think he had.

As the red sun climbed above the horizon Ch'aka appeared on top of the dunes, shaking with rage.

"Who did it?" he screamed. "Who came in night?" He stalked among them, glaring right and left, and no one stirred except to draw away from his stamping feet. "Who did it?" he shouted again as he came near the spot where Jason lay.

Five slaves pointed silently at Jason, and Ijale shuddered and drew away from him.

Cursing their betrayal, Jason sprang up and ran from the whistling club. He had the sharpened horn in his hand but knew better than to try and stand up to Ch'aka in open combat; there had to be another way. He looked back quickly and saw his enemy still following, and in doing so he narrowly missed tripping over the outstretched leg of a slave.

They were all against him! They were all against each other, and no man was safe from any other man's hand. He ran free of the slaves and scrambled to the top of a shifting dune, pulling himself up the steep slope by clutching at the coarse grass. He turned at the top and kicked sand into Ch'aka's face, trying to blind him, but the slave-master swung down his crossbow and notched a steel quarrel, and Jason had to run. Ch'aka chased him again, panting heavily.

Jason was tiring now, and he knew this was the best time

to launch a counterattack. The slaves were out of sight, and it would be a battle between only the two of them. Scrambling up a slope of broken rock, he reversed himself suddenly and leaped back down. Ch'aka was taken by surprise and had his club only half raised when Jason was upon him, and he swung wildly. Jason ducked under the blow and used Ch'aka's momentum to help throw him as he grabbed the club arm and pulled.

Face down, the armored man crashed against the stones, and Jason was straddling his back even as he fell, clutching for his chin. He lacerated his fingers on a jagged tooth necklace, then grasped the man's thick beard and pulled back. For a single long instant, before he could write free and roll over, Ch'aka's head was stretched back, and in that instant Jason plunged the sharp horn deep into the soft flesh of the throat. Hot blood burst over his hand and Ch'aka shuddered horribly under him, and died.

Jason climbed to his feet, suddenly exhausted. He was alone with his victim. The cold wind swept about them, carrying the rustling grains of sand, chilling the sweat on his body. Sighing once, he wiped his bloody hands on the sand and began to strip the corpse. Thick straps held the shell helmet over the dead man's head, and when he unknotted them and pulled the helmet away he saw that Ch'aka was well past middle age. There was some grey in his beard, and his scraggly hair was completely grey; his face and balding head were pallid white from being concealed under the helmet.

It took a long time to get the wrappings and armor off and tie them on himself, but it was finally done. Under the skin and claw wrappings on Ch'aka's feet were Jason's boots, filthy but undamaged, and Jason drew them on happily. When at last, after scouring the helmet out with sand, he had strapped it on, Ch'aka was reborn. The corpse on the sand was just another dead slave. Jason scraped a shallow grave, interred the body, and covered it.

Then, slung about with weapons, bags, and crossbow, the club in his hand, he stalked back to the waiting slaves. As soon as he appeared they scrambled to their feet and formed a line. Jason saw Ijale looking at him worriedly, trying to discover who had won the battle.

"Score one for the visiting team," he called out, and she gave him a small, frightened smile and turned away. "About

43

face all, and head back the way we came. There is a new day dawning for you slaves. I know you don't believe this yet, but there are some big changes in store."

He whistled while he strolled after the line and chewed happily on the first *kreno* that was found.

CHAPTER SIX

That evening they built a fire on the beach and Jason sat with his back to the safety of the sea. He took his helmet off—the thing was giving him a headache—and called Ijale over to him.

"I hear Ch'aka. I obey."

She ran hurriedly to him and flopped onto the sand, pulling open her rawhide wrappings.

"What an opinion of men you have!" Jason exploded. "Sit up—all I want to do is talk to you. And my name is Jason, not Ch'aka."

"Yes, Ch'aka," she said, darting a quick glance at his exposed face, then turning away. He grumbled, and pushed the basket of *krenoj* over to her.

"I can see where it is not going to be an easy thing changing this social setup. Tell me, do you or any of the others ever have any desire to be free?"

"What is free?"

"Well—I suppose that answers my question. Free is what you are when you are not a slave, or a slave owner, free to go where you want and do what you want."

"I wouldn't like that." She shivered. "Who would take care of me? How could I find any *krenoj*? It takes many people together to find *krenoj*—one alone would starve."

"If you are free you can combine with other free people and look for *krenoj* together."

"That is stupid. Whoever found would eat and not share unless a master made him. I like to eat."

Jason rasped his sprouting beard. "We all like to eat, but that doesn't mean we have to be slaves. But I can see that unless there are some radical changes in this environment I am not going to have much luck in freeing anyone, and I had better take all the precautions of a Ch'aka to see that I can stay alive."

He picked up his club and stalked off into the darkness, silently circling the camp until he found a good-sized knoll with smooth sides. Working by touch he pulled the little pegs from their bag and planted them in rows, carefully laying the leather strings in their forked tops. The ends of the strings were fastened to delicately balanced steel bells that tinkled at the slightest touch. Thus protected, he lay down in the center of his warning spiderweb and spent a restless night, half awake, waiting tensely for the bells to ring.

In the morning the march continued. They came to the barrier cairn, and when the slaves stopped Jason urged them past it. They did this happily, looking forward to witnessing a good fight for possession of the violated territory. Their hopes were justified when later in the day the other row of slaves was seen far off to the right, and a figure detached itself and ran towards them.

"Hate you, Ch'aka!" Fasimba shouted as he ran up, only this time he meant what he said. "Coming on my ground, I kill you!"

"Not yet," Jason called out. "And hate you, Fasimba, sorry I forgot the formalities. I don't want any of your land, and the old treaty of whatever it is still holds. I just want to talk to you."

Fasimba stopped, but kept his stone hammer ready, very suspicious. "You got new voice, Ch'aka."

"I got new Ch'aka; old Ch'aka now pushing up the daisies. I want to trade back a slave from you and then we'll go."

"Ch'aka fight hard. You must be good fighter, Ch'aka." He shook his hammer angrily. "Not as good as me, Ch'aka!"

"You're the tops, Fasimba; nine slaves out of ten want you for a master. Look, can't we get to the point, then I'll get my mob out of here." He looked at the row of approaching slaves, trying to pick out Mikah. "I want back the slave who had the hole in his head. I'll give you two slaves in trade, your choice. What do you say to that?"

"Good trade, Ch'aka. You pick one of mine, take the best, I'll take two of yours. But hole-in-head gone. Too much trouble. Talk all the time. I got sore foot from kicking him. Got rid of him."

"Did you kill him?"

"Don't waste slave. Traded him to the *d'zertanoj*. Got arrows. You want arrows?"

"Not this time, Fasimba, but thanks for the information." He rooted around in a pouch and pulled out a *kreno*. "Here, have something to eat."

46

"Where you get poisoned *kreno*?" Fasimba asked with unconcealed interest. "I could use a poisoned *kreno*."

"This isn't poisoned, it's perfectly edible, or at least as edible as these things ever are."

Fasimba laughed. "You pretty funny Ch'aka. I give you one arrow for poisoned *kreno*."

"You're on," Jason said, throwing the *kreno* to the ground between them. "But I tell you it is perfectly good."

"That's what I tell man I give it to. I got good use for a poisoned *kreno*." He threw an arrow into the sand away from them and grabbed up the vegetable as he left.

When Jason picked up the arrow it bent, and he saw that it was rusted almost completely in two and that the break had been craftily covered by clay. "That's all right," he called after the retreating slaver. "Just wait until your friend eats the *kreno*."

They continued their march, first back to the boundary cairn with the suspicious Fasimba dogging their steps. Only after Jason and his band had passed the border did the others return to their normal foraging.

Then began the long walk to the borders of the inland desert. Since they had to search for *krenoj* as they went, it took them the better part of three days to reach their destination. Jason merely started the line in the right direction, but as soon as he was out of sight of the sea he had only a rough idea of the correct course. However, he did not confide his ignorance to the slaves and they marched steadily on, along what was obviously a well-known route to them. Along the way they collected and consumed a good number of *krenoj*, found two wells from which they refilled the skin bags, and pointed out a huddled animal sitting by a hole that Jason, to their unvoiced disgust, managed to miss completely with a bolt from the crossbow. On the morning of the third day Jason saw a line of demarcation on the flattened horizon, and before the midday meal they came to a sea of billowing, bluish-grey sand.

The ending of what he had been accustomed to thinking of as the desert was startling. Beneath their feet were sand and gravel while occasional shrubs managed a sickly existence, as did some grass and the life-giving *krenoj*. Animals as well as men lived here and, ruthless though survival was, they were at least alive. In the wastes ahead no life was visible or possible, though there seemed to be no doubt that

47

the *d'zertanoj* lived there. This must mean that though it looked unlimited—as Ijale believed it to be—there were probably arable lands on the other side. Mountains as well, if they weren't just clouds, since a line of grey peaks could just be made out on the distant horizon.

"Where do we find the *d'zertanoj*?" Jason asked the nearest slave, who merely scowled and looked away. Jason was having a problem with discipline. The slaves would not do a thing he asked unless he kicked them. Their conditioning had been so thorough that an order unaccompanied by a kick just wasn't an order, and his continued reluctance to impose the physical coercion with the spoken command was being taken as a sign of weakness. Already some of the burlier slaves were licking their lips and sizing him up. His efforts to improve the life of the slaves were being blocked completely by the slaves themselves. With a muttered curse at the continued obduracy of these creatures, Jason kicked the man with the toe of his boot.

"Find them there by big rock," was the immediate response.

There was a dark spot at the desert's edge in the indicated direction, and when they approached this Jason saw that it was an outcropping of rock that had been built up with a wall of bricks and boulders to a uniform height. A good number of men could be concealed behind that wall, and he was not going to risk his precious slaves or even more precious skin anywhere near it. At his shout the line halted and sank down on the sand while he stalked a few meters in front, settling his club in his hand and suspiciously examining the structure.

That there were unseen watchers was proved when a man appeared from around the corner and walked slowly towards Jason. He was dressed in loose-fitting robes and carried a basket on one arm, and when he had reached a point roughly halfway between Jason and the rock he had just quitted, he halted and sat crosslegged in the sand, the basket at his side. Jason looked carefully in all directions, and decided the situation was safe enough. There were no places of concealment where armed men might have hidden, and he had no fear of the one man alone. Club ready, he walked out and stopped a full three paces from the other.

"Welcome, Ch'aka," the man said. "I was afraid we
48

wouldn't be seeing you again after that little . . . difficulty we had."

He remained seated while he talked, stroking the few strands of his scraggly beard. His head was shaved smooth and was as sunburned and leathery as the rest of his face, the most prominent feature of which was a magnificent prow of a nose that terminated in flaring nostrils and was used as sturdy support for a pair of handsome sunglasses. They appeared to be carved completely of bone and fitted tightly to the face; their flat, solid fronts were cut with thin transverse slashes. This sort of eye protection could only have been for weak eyes, and the network of wrinkles suggested that the man was quite old and would present no danger to Jason.

"I want something," Jason said in straightforward, Ch'akaish manner.

"A new voice and a new Ch'aka—I bid you welcome. The old one was a dog, and I hope he died in great pain when you killed him. Now sit, friend Ch'aka, and drink with me." He carefully uncovered the basket and removed a stone crock and two crockery mugs.

"Where you get poison drink?" Jason asked, remembering his local manners. This *d'zertano* was a smart one; he had been able to tell instantly from Jason's voice that there had been a change in identity. "And what your name?"

"Epidon," the ancient said as, not insulted, he put the drinking apparatus back into the basket. "What is it that you want? Within reason, that is. We always need slaves and we are always willing to trade."

"I want slave you got. I trade you two for one."

The seated man smiled coldly from behind the shelter of his nose. "It is not necessary to talk as ungrammatically as the coastal barbarians, since I can tell by your accent that you are a man of education. What slave is it that you want?"

"The one you just received from Fasimba. He belongs to me." Jason abandoned his linguistic ruse and put himself even more on guard, taking a quick look around at the empty sands. This dried-up old bird was a lot brighter than he looked, and Jason would have to stay on guard.

"Is that all you want?" Edipon asked.

"All I can think of at this moment. You produce this slave and maybe we can talk some more business."

Edipon's laugh had very dirty overtones, and Jason sprang

49

back when the oldster put two fingers into his mouth and whistled shrilly between them. There was the rustle of shifting sand, and Jason wheeled to see men apparently climbing out of the empty desert, pushing back wooden covers over which the sand had been smoothed. There were six of them with shields and clubs, and Jason cursed his stupidity at meeting Edipon on a spot of the other's choosing. He swung his club behind him, but the old man was already scampering for the safety of the rock. Jason howled in anger and ran at the nearest man, who was still only halfway out of his hiding place. The man took Jason's blow on his upraised shield and was toppled back into the pit by the force of it. Jason ran on, but another was ahead of him, swinging his own war club in readiness. There was no way around, so Jason ran into him at full speed with all of his pendant teeth and horns gnashing and clattering. The man fell back under the attack and Jason split his shield with his club, and would have done further damage had the other men not arrived at that moment and he had to face them.

It was a brief and wicked battle, with Jason giving just a little more than he received. Two of the attackers were down and a third was holding his cracked head when the weight of numbers carried Jason to the ground. He called to his slaves for aid, then cursed them when they only remained seated, while his arms were pinioned with rope and his weapons stripped from his body. One of the victors waved to the slaves who now docilely marched into the desert. Jason was dragged, snarling with rage, in the same direction.

There was a wide opening in the desert-facing side of the wall, and once through it Jason's anger instantly vanished. Here was one of the *caroj* that Ijale had told him about : there could be no doubt of it. He could now understand how, to her uneducated eye, there could exist an uncertainty as to whether the thing was an animal or not. The vehicle was a good ten meters long, and was shaped roughly like a boat; it bore on the front a large and obviously false animal head covered with fur, and resplendent with rows of carved teeth and glistening crystal eyes. Hide coverings and not very realistic legs were hung on the thing, surely not enough camouflage to fool a civilized six-year-old. This sort of disguise might be good enough to take in the ignorant savages, but the same civilized child would recognize this as a vehicle as soon as he saw the six large wheels underneath. They were cut with deep treads and made from some resilient-looking substance. No motive power was visible, but Jason almost hooted with joy at the noticeable smell of burnt fuel. This crude-looking contrivance had some artificial source of power, which might be the product of a local industrial revolution, or might have been purchased from off-world traders. Either possibility offered the chance of eventual escape from this nameless planet.

The slaves, some of them cringing with terror of the unknown, were kicked up the gangplank and into the *caro*. Four of the huskies who had subdued and bound Jason carried him up and dumped him onto the deck, where he lay quietly and examined what could be seen of the desert vehicle's mechanism. A post projected from the front of the deck, and one of the men fitted what could only be a tiller handle over the squared top of it. If this monolithic apparatus steered with the front pair of wheels it must be driven with the rear ones, so Jason flopped around on the deck until he could look towards the stern. A cabin, the width of the deck, was situated here, windowless and with a single inset door fitted with a grand selection of locks and bolts. Any doubts that this was the engine room was dispelled by the black metal smokestack that rose up through the cabin roof.

"We are leaving," Edipon screeched, and waved his thin arms in the air. "Bring in the entranceway. Narsisi, stand forward to indicate the way to the *caro*. Now—all pray as I go into the shrine to induce the sacred powers to move us towards Putl'ko." He started towards the cabin, then stopped to point to one of the club bearers. "Erebo, you lazy sod, did you remember to fill the watercup of the gods this time, for they grow thirsty?"

"I filled it, I filled it," Erebo muttered, chewing on a looted *kreno*.

Preparations made, Edipon went into the recessed doorway and pulled a concealing curtain over it. There was much clanking and rattling as the locks and bolts were opened and he let himself inside. Within a few minutes a black cloud of greasy smoke rolled out of the smokestack and was whipped away by the wind. Almost an hour passed before the sacred powers were ready to move, and they announced their willingness to proceed by screaming and blowing their white breath up in the air. Four of the slaves screamed counterpoint and fainted, while the rest looked as if they would be happier dead.

Jason had had some experience with primitive machines before, so the safety valve on the boiler came as no great surprise. He was also prepared when the vehicle shuddered and began to move slowly out into the desert. From the amount of smoke and the quantity of steam escaping from under the stern he didn't think the engine was very efficient, but primitive as it was it moved the *caro* and its load of passengers across the sand at a creeping yet steady pace.

More screams came from the slaves, and a few tried to leap over the side, but they were clubbed down. The robe-wrapped *d'zertanoj* were firmly working their way through the ranks of the captives, pouring ladlefuls of dark liquid down their throats. Some of the captives were slumped unconscious, or were dead, though the chances were better that they were merely unconscious, since there was no reason for their captors to kill them after going to such lengths to get them in the first place. Jason believed this, but the terrified slaves did not have the solace of his philosophy, so struggled on, thinking that they were fighting for their lives.

When Jason's turn came he did not submit meekly, in spite of his beliefs, and managed to bite some fingers and kick one man in the stomach before they sat on him, held his nose, and poured a measure of the burning liquid down his throat. It hurt and he felt dizzy, and he tried to will himself to throw up, but this was the last thing that he remembered.

CHAPTER SEVEN

"Drink some more of this," the voice said, and cold water splashed on Jason's face and some of it trickled down his throat, making him cough. Something hard was pressing into his back and his wrists hurt. Memory seeped back slowly —the fight, the capture, and the potion that had been forced upon him. When he opened his eyes he saw a flickering yellow lamp overhead, hung from a chain. He blinked at it and tried to gather enough energy to sit up. A familiar face swam in front of the light and Jason squinted his eyes at it and groaned.

"Is that you, Mikah—or are you just part of a nightmare?"

"There is no escape from justice, Jason. It is I, and I have some grave questions to put to you."

Jason groaned again. "You're real, all right. Even in a nightmare I wouldn't dare dream up any lines like that. But before the questions, how about telling me a thing or two about the local setup? You should know something, since you have been a slave of the *d'zertanoj* longer than I have." Jason realized that the pain in his wrists came from heavy iron shackles. A chain passed through them and was stapled to a thick wooden bar on which his head had been resting. "Why the chains—and what is the local hospitality like?"

Mikah resisted the invitation to impart any vital information and returned irresistibly to his own topic.

"When I saw you last you were a slave of Ch'aka, and tonight you were brought in with the other slaves of Ch'aka and chained to the bar while you were unconscious. There was an empty place next to mine and I told them I would tend you if they placed you there, and they did so. Now there is something I must know. Before they stripped you, I saw that you were wearing the armor and helmet of Ch'aka. Where is he—what happened to him?"

"Me Ch'aka," Jason rasped, and burst out coughing from the dryness in his throat. He took a long drink of water from the bowl. "You sound very vindictive, Mikah, you old fraud. Where is all the turn-the-other-cheek stuff now? Don't tell me you could possibly hate the man just because he hit you on the head, fractured your skull, and sold you down the river as a slave reject? In case you have been brooding over this injustice you can now be cheered, because the evil Ch'aka is no more. He is buried in the trackless wastes, and after all the applicants were sifted out I got the job."

"You killed him?"

"In a word—yes. And don't think that it was easy, for he had all the advantages and I possessed only my native ingenuity, which luckily proved to be enough. It was touch and go for a while, because when I tried to assassinate him in his sleep—"

"You *what*?" Mikah interrupted.

"Got to him at night. You don't think anyone in his right mind would tackle a monster like that face to face, do you? Though it ended up that way, since he had some neat gadgets for keeping track of people in the dark. Briefly, we fought, I won, I became Ch'aka, though my reign was neither long nor noble. I followed you as far as the desert, where I was neatly trapped by a shrewd old bird by the name of Edipon, who demoted me back to the ranks and took away all my slaves as well. Now that's my story. So tell me yours—where we are, what goes on here—"

"Assassin! Slaveholder!" Mikah reared back as far as he could under the restraint of the chain, and pointed the finger of judgment at Jason. "Two more charges must be added to your role of infamy. I sicken myself, Jason, that I could ever have felt sympathy for you and tried to help you. I will still help you, but only to stay alive so that you can be taken back to Cassylia for trial and execution."

"I like that example of fair and impartial justice—trial *and* execution." Jason coughed again and drained the bowl of water. "Didn't you ever hear of presumed innocence until proven guilt? It happens to be the mainstay of all jurisprudence. And how could you possibly justify trying me on Cassylia for actions that occurred on this planet—actions that aren't crimes here? That's like taking a cannibal away from his tribe and executing him for anthropophagy."

"What would be wrong with that? The eating of human flesh is a crime so loathsome I shudder to think of it. Of course a man who does that must be executed."

"If he slips in the back door and eats one of your relatives you certainly have grounds for action. But not if he
54

joins the rest of his jolly tribe for a good roast of enemy. Don't you see the obvious point here—that human conduct can be judged only in relation to its environment? Conduct is relative. The cannibal in his society is just as moral as the churchgoer in yours."

"Blasphemer! A crime is a crime! There are moral laws that stand above all human society."

"Oh, no, there aren't. That's just the point where your medieval morality breaks down. All laws and ideas are historical and relative, *not* absolute. They are relevant to their particular time and place; taken out of context they lose their importance. Within the context of this grubby society, I acted in a most straightforward and honest manner. I attempted to assassinate my master—which is the only way an ambitious boy can get ahead in this hard world, and which was undoubtedly the way Ch'aka himself got the job in the first place. Assassination didn't work, but combat did, and the results were the same. Once in power, I took good care of my slaves, though of course they didn't appreciate it, since they didn't want good care : they only wanted my job, that being the law of the land. The only thing I really did wrong was not to live up to my obligations as a slaveholder and keep them marching up and down the beaches forever. Instead, I came looking for you and was trapped and broken back to slavery, where I belong for pulling such a stupid trick."

The door crashed open and harsh sunlight streamed into the windowless building. "On your feet, slaves!" a *d'zertano* shouted in through the opening.

A chorus of groans and shufflings broke out as the men stirred to life. Jason could see now that he was one of twenty slaves shackled to the long bar, apparently the entire trunk of a good-sized tree. The man chained at the far end seemed to be a leader of sorts, for he cursed and goaded the others to life. When they were all standing he snapped his commands in a hectoring tone.

"Come on, come on! First come best food. And don't forget your bowls. Put them away so they can't drop out, remember nothing to eat or drink all day unless you have a bowl. And let's work together today, everyone pull his weight, that's the only way to do it. That goes for all you men, especially you new men. Give them a day's work here and they give you a day's food ..."

"Oh, shut up !" someone shouted.

". . . and you can't complain about that," the man went on, unperturbed. "Now altogether . . . *one* . . . bend down and get your hands around the bar, get a good grip and . . . *two* . . . lift it clear of the ground, that's the way. And . . . *three* . . . stand up, and out the door we go."

They shuffled out into the sunlight and the cold wind of dawn bit through the Pyrran coverall and the remnants of Ch'aka's leather trappings that Jason had been allowed to keep. His captors had torn off the claw-studded feet but had not bothered the wrappings underneath, so they hadn't found his boots. This was the only bright spot on an otherwise unlimited vista of blackest gloom. Jason tried to be thankful for small blessings, but he could only shiver. As soon as possible this situation had to be changed, for he had already served his term as slave on this backward planet and was cut out for better things.

On order, the slaves dropped their bar against the wall of the yard and sat upon it. Presenting their bowls like scruffy penitents, they accepted dippers of lukewarm soup from another slave who pushed along a wheeled tub of the stuff : he was chained to the tub. Jason's appetite vanished when he tasted the sludge. It was *kreno* soup, and the desert tubers tasted even worse—he hadn't thought it was possible—when served up in a broth. But survival was more important than fastidiousness, so he gulped the evil stuff down.

Breakfast over, they marched out the gate into another compound, and fascinated interest displaced all of Jason's concerns. In the center of the yard was a large capstan into which the first group of slaves were already fitting the end of their bar. Jason's group, and the two others, shuffled into position and placed their bars, making a four-spoked wheel out of the capstan. An overseer shouted and the slaves groaned and threw their weight against the bars until they shuddered and began to turn; then trudging slowly, they kept the wheel moving.

Once this slogging labor was under way, Jason turned his attention to the crude mechanism they were powering. A vertical shaft from the capstan turned a creaking wooden wheel that set a series of leather belts in motion. Some of them vanished through openings into a large stone building, while the strongest strap of all turned the rocker arm of what could only be a counterbalanced pump. This all seemed like a highly inefficient way to go about pumping water, since there must be natural springs and lakes somewhere around. The pungent smell that filled the yard was hauntingly familiar, and Jason had just reached the conclusion that water couldn't be the object of their labors when a throaty gurgling came from the standpipe of the pump and a thick black stream bubbled out.

"Petroleum—of course!" Jason said out loud. Then when the overseer gave him an ugly look and cracked his whip menacingly, he bent his attention to pushing.

This was the secret of the *d'zertanoj*, and the source of their power. Hills towered above the surrounding walls and mountains were visible nearby. But the captured slaves had been drugged so they would not even know in which direction they had been brought to this hidden site, or how long the trip was. Here in this guarded valley they labored to pump the crude oil that their masters used to power their big desert wagons. Or did they use crude oil for this? The petroleum was gurgling out in a heavy stream now, and was running down an open trough that disappeared through the wall into the same building as the turning belts. What barbaric devilishness went on in there? A thick chimney crowned the building and produced clouds of black smoke, while from the various openings in the wall came a tremendous stench that threatened to lift the top off his head.

At the same moment that he realized what was going on in the building, a guarded door was opened and Edipon came out, blowing his sizeable nose in a scrap of rag. The creaking wheel turned, and when its rotation brought Jason around again he called out to him.

"Hey, Edipon, come over here. I want to talk to you. I'm the former Ch'aka, in case you don't recognize me out of uniform."

Edipon gave him one look, then turned away, dabbing at his nose. It was obvious that slaves held no interest for him, no matter what their position had been before their fall. The slave driver ran over with a roar, raising his whip, while the slow rotation of the wheel carried Jason away. He shouted back over his shoulder.

"Listen to me—I know a lot, and can help you." Only a turned back was an answer, and the whip was already whistling down.

It was time for the hard sell. "You had better hear me—

because I know that *what comes out first is best.* Yeow!"
This last was involuntary as the whip landed.

Jason's words were without meaning to the slaves as well as to the overseer, who was raising his whip for another blow, but their impact on Edipon was as dramatic as if he had stepped on a hot coal. He shuddered to a halt and wheeled about, and even at this distance Jason could see that a sickly grey tone had replaced the normal brown color of his skin.

"Stop the wheel!" Edipon shouted.

This unexpected command drew the startled attention of everyone. The gape-mouthed overseer lowered his whip while the slaves stumbled and halted and the wheel groaned to a stop. In the sudden silence Edipon's steps echoed loudly as he ran to Jason, halting a hand's breadth away, his lips drawn back from his teeth with tension as if he were prepared to bite.

"What was that you said?" He hurled the words at Jason while his fingers half plucked a knife from his belt.

Jason smiled, looking and acting calmer than he felt. His barb had gone home, but unless he proceeded carefully so would Edipon's knife—into Jason's stomach. This was obviously a very sensitive topic.

"You heard what I said—and I don't think you want me to repeat it in front of all these strangers. I know what happens here because I come from a place far away where we do this kind of thing all the time. I can help you. I can show you how to get more of the best, and how to make your *caroj* work better. Just try me. Only unchain me from this bar first and let's get to some place private where we can have a nice chat."

Edipon's thoughts were obvious. He chewed his lip and looked hotly at Jason, fingering the edge of his knife. Jason returned a smile of pure innocence and tapped his fingers happily on the bar, just marking time while he waited to be released. But in spite of the cold there was a rivulet of sweat trickling down his spine. He was gambling everything on Edipon's intelligence, believing that the man's curiosity would overcome the immediate desire to silence the slave who knew so much about things so secret, hoping that he would remember that slaves could always be killed, and that it wouldn't hurt to ask a few questions first. Curiosity won, and the knife dropped back into the sheath while Jason let his breath out in a relieved sigh. It had been entirely too close, even for a professional gambler; his own life on the board was a little higher stakes than he enjoyed playing for.

"Release him from the bar and bring him to me," Edipon ordered, then strode away in agitation. The other slaves watched wide-eyed as the blacksmith was rushed out, and with much confusion and shouted orders Jason's chain was cut from the bar where it joined the heavy staple.

"What are you doing?" Mikah asked, and one of the guards backhanded him to the ground. Jason merely smiled and touched his finger to his lips as his chain was released and they led him away. He was free from bondage, and he would stay that way if he could convince Edipon that he would be of better use in some capacity other than dumb labor.

The room they led him to contained the first touches of decoration or self-indulgence that he had seen on this planet. The furniture was carefully constructed, with an occasional bit of carving to brighten it, and there was a woven cover on the bed. Edipon stood by a table, tapping his fingers nervously on the dark polished surface.

"Lock him up," he ordered the guards, and Jason was secured to a sturdy ringbolt that projected from the wall. As soon as the guards were gone Edipon stood in front of Jason and drew his knife. "Tell me what you know, or I will kill you at once."

"My past is an open book to you, Edipon. I come from a land where we know all the secrets of nature."

"What is the name of this land? Are you a spy from Appsala?"

"I couldn't very well be, since I have never heard of the place." Jason pulled at his lower lip, wondering just how intelligent Edipon was, and just how frank he could be with him. This was no time to get tangled up in lies about the planetary geography : it might be best to try him on a small dose of the truth.

"If I told you I came from another planet, another world in the sky among the stars, would you believe me?"

"Perhaps. There are many old legends that our forefathers came from a world beyond the sky, but I have always dismissed them as religious drivel, fit only for women."

"In this case the girls happen to be right. Your planet was settled by men whose ships crossed the emptiness of space as your *caroj* pass over the desert. Your people have forgotten

59

about that, and have lost the science and knowledge you once had, but on other worlds the knowledge is still held."

"Madness!"

"Not at all. It is science, though many times confused as being the same thing. I'll prove my point. You know that I could never have been inside of your mysterious building out there, and I imagine you can be sure no one has told me its secrets. Yet I'll bet that I can describe fairly accurately what is in there—not from seeing the machinery, but from knowing what must be done to oil in order to get the products you need. You want to hear?"

"Proceed," Edipon said, sitting on a corner of the table and balancing the knife loosely in his palm.

"I don't know what you call it, the device, but in the trade it is a pot still used for fractional distillation. Your crude oil runs into a tank of some kind, and you pipe it from there to a retort, some big vessel that you can seal airtight. Once it is closed, you light a fire under the thing and try to get all the oil to an even temperature. A gas rises from the oil and you take it off through a pipe and run it through a condenser, probably more pipe with water running over it. Then you put a bucket under the open end of the pipe and out of it drips the juice that you burn in your *caroj* to make them move."

Edipon's eyes opened wider and wider while Jason talked, until they seemed almost bulging from his head. "Demon!" he screeched, and tottered towards Jason with the knife extended. "You couldn't have seen, not through stone walls. Only my family have seen, no others—I'll swear to that!"

"Keep cool, Edipon. I told you that we have been doing this stuff for years in my country." He balanced on one foot, ready for a kick at the knife in case the old man's nerves did not settle down. "I'm not out to steal your secrets. In fact, they are pretty small potatoes where I come from, where every farmer has a still for cooking up his own mash and saving on taxes. I'll bet I can even put in some improvements for you, sight unseen. How do you monitor the temperature on your cooking brew? Do you have thermometers?"

"What are thermometers?" Edipon asked, forgetting the knife for the moment, drawn on by the joy of technical discussion.

"That's what I thought. I can see where your bootleg joy-juice is going to take a big jump in quality, if you have

60

anyone here who can do some simple glass-blowing. Though it might be easier to rig up a coiled bi-metallic strip. You're trying to boil off your various fractions, and unless you keep an even and controlled temperature you are going to have a mixed brew. The thing you want for your engines are the most volatile fractions, the liquids that boil off first, like gasoline and benzine. After that you raise the temperature and collect kerosene for your lamps, and so forth right on down the line until you have a nice mass of tar to pave your roads with. How does that sound to you?"

Edipon had forced himself into calmness, though a jumping muscle in his cheek betrayed his inner tension. "What you have described is the truth, though you were wrong on some small things. But I am not interested in your thermometer nor in improving our water-of-power. It has been good enough for my family for generations and it is good enough for me."

"I suppose you think that line is original?"

"But there is something that you might be able to do that would bring you rich rewards," Edipon went on. "We can be generous when needs be. You have seen our *caroj* and ridden on one, and seen me go into the shrine to intercede with the sacred powers to make us move. Can you tell me what power moves the *caroj*?"

"I hope this is the final exam, Edipon, because you are stretching my powers of extrapolation. Stripping away the 'shrines' and 'sacred powers', I would say that you go into the engine room to do a piece of work with very little praying involved. There could be a number of ways of moving those vehicles, but let's think of the simplest. This is top of the head now, so no penalties if I miss any of the fine points. Internal combustion is out. I doubt if you have the technoloy to handle it, plus the fact there was a lot of do about the water tank and it took you almost an hour to get under way. That sounds as if you were getting up a head of steam —the safety valve! I forgot about that.

"So it is steam. You go in, lock the door, of course, then open a couple of valves until the fuel drips into the firebox, then you light it. Maybe you have a pressure gauge, or maybe you just wait until the safety valve pops to tell you if you have a head of steam. Which can be dangerous, since a sticking valve could blow the whole works right over the mountain. Once you have the steam, you crack a valve to let it into the cylinders and get the thing moving. After that you just enjoy the trip, of course making sure that the water is feeding to your boiler all right, that your pressure stays up, your fire is hot enough, all your bearings are lubricated, and the rest . . ."

Jason looked on astounded as Edipon did a little jig around the room, holding his robe above his bony knees. Bouncing with excitement, he jabbed his knife into the table top and rushed over to Jason and grabbed him by the shoulders, shaking him so that his chain rattled.

"Do you know what you have done?" he asked excitedly. "Do you know what you have said?"

"I know well enough. Does this mean that I have passed the exam and that you will listen to me now? Was I right?"

"I don't know if you are right or not; I have never seen the inside of one of the Appsalan devil-boxes." He danced around the room again. "You know more about their—what do you call it?—*engine*, than I do. I have only spent my life tending them and cursing the people of Appsala who keep the secret from us. But you will reveal it to us! We will build our own engines, and if they want water-of-power they will have to pay dearly for it."

"Would you mind being a little bit clearer," Jason asked. "I have never heard anything so confused in all my life."

"I will show you, man from a far world, and you will reveal the Appsalan secrets to us. I see the dawn of a new day for Putl'ko arriving."

He opened the door and shouted for the guards, and for his son, Narsisi. The latter arrived as they were unlocking Jason, who recognized him as the same droopy-eyed, sleepy-looking *d'zertano* who had been helping Edipon to drive their ungainly vehicle.

"Seize this chain, my son, and keep your club ready to kill this slave if he makes any attempt to escape. Otherwise, do not harm him, for he is very valuable. Come."

Narsisi tugged on the chain, but Jason only dug his heels in and did not move. They looked at him, astonished.

"Just a few things before we go. The man who is to bring the new day to Putl'ko is not a slave. Let us get that straight before this operation goes any further. We'll work out something with chains or guards so I can't escape, but the slavery thing is out."

62

"But—you are not one of us, therefore you must be a slave."

"I've just added a third category to your social order : employee. Though reluctant, I am still an employee, skilled labor, and I intend to be treated that way. Figure it out for yourself. Kill a slave, and what do you lose? Very little, if there is another slave in the pens that can push in the same place. But kill me, and what do you get? Brains on your club—and they do you no good at all there."

"Does he mean I can't kill him?" Narsisi asked his father, looking puzzled as well as sleepy.

"No, he doesn't mean that," Edipon said. "He means if we kill him there is no one else who can do the work he is to do for us. But I do not like it. There are only slaves and slavers ! anything else is against the natural order. But he has us trapped between *satano* and the sandstorm, so we must allow him some freedom. Bring the slave now—I mean the employee—and we will see if he can do the things he has promised. If he does not, *I* will have the pleasure of killing him, because I do not like his revolutionary ideas."

They marched single file to a locked and guarded building with immense doors, which were pulled open to reveal the massive forms of seven *caroj*.

"Look at them !" Edipon exclaimed, and pulled at his nose. "The finest and most beautiful of constructions, striking fear into our enemies' hearts, carrying us fleetly across the sands, bearing on their backs immense loads, and only three of the damned things are able to move."

"Engine trouble?" Jason asked lightly.

Edipon cursed and fumed under his breath, and led the way to an inner courtyard where stood four immense black boxes painted with death heads, splintered bones, fountains of blood, and cabalistic symbols, all of a sinister appearance.

"Those swine in Appsala take our water-of-power and give nothing in return. Oh yes, they let us use their engines, but after running for a few months the cursed things stop and will not go again, then we must bring them back to the city to exchange for a new one, and pay again and again."

"A nice racket," Jason said, looking at the sealed covering on the engines. "Why don't you just crack into them and fix them yourself? They can't be very complex."

"That is death !" Edipon gasped, and both *d'zertanoj* recoiled from the boxes at the thought. "We have tried that, in my father's father's day, for we are not superstitious like the slaves, and we know that these are man-made not god-made. However, the tricky serpents of Appsala hide their secrets with immense cunning. If any attempt is made to break the covering, horrible death leaks out and fills the air. Men who breathe the air die, and even those who are only touched by it develop immense blisters and die in pain. The men of Appsala laughed when this happened to our people, and after that they raised the price even higher."

Jason circled one of the boxes, examining it with interest, trailing Narsisi behind him at the end of the chain. The thing was higher than his head and almost twice as long. A heavy shaft emerged through openings on opposite sides, probably the power takeoff for the wheels. Through an opening in the side he could see inset handles and two small colored disks, and above these were three funnel-shaped openings painted like mouths. By standing on tiptoe, Jason could look on top, but there was only a flanged, sooty opening there that must be for attaching a smokestack. There was only one more opening, a smallish one in the rear, and no other controls on the garish container

"I'm beginning to get the picture, but you will have to tell me how to work the controls."

"Death before that!" Narsisi shouted. "Only my family —"

"Will you shut up!" Jason shouted back. "Remember? You're not allowed to browbeat the help any more. There are no secrets here. Not only that, but I probably know more about this thing than you do, just by looking at it. Oil, water, and fuel go in these three openings, you poke a light in somewhere, probably in that smoky hole under the controls, and open one of those valves for fuel supply; another one is to make the engine go slower and faster, and the third is for your water feed. The disks are indicators of some kind." Narsisi paled and stepped back. "So now keep still while I talk to your dad."

"It is as you say," Edipon said. "The mouths must always be filled, and woe betide if they go empty; for the powers will halt, or worse. Fire goes in here, as you guessed, and when the green finger comes forward this lever may be turned for motion. The next is for great speed, or for going slow. The very last is under the sign of the red finger, which when it points indicates need, and the handle must be turned and held until the finger retires. White breath comes from the opening in back. That is all there is."

"About what I expected," Jason muttered, and examined the container wall, rapping it with his knuckles until it boomed. "They give you the minimum of controls to run the thing, so you won't learn anything about the basic principles involved. Without the theory, you would never know what the handles control, or that the green indicator comes out when you have operating pressure, and the red one when the water level is low in the boiler. Very neat. And the whole thing sealed up in a can and booby-trapped in case you have any ideas of going into business for yourself. The cover sounds as if it is double-walled, and from your description I would say that it has one of the vesicant war gases, like mustard gas, sealed inside there in liquid form. Anyone who tries to cut their way in will quickly forget their ambitions after a dose of that. Yet there must be a way to get inside the case and service the engine; they aren't just going to throw them away after a few months' use. And considering the level of technology displayed by this monstrosity, I should be able to find the tricks and get around any other built-in traps. I think I'll take the job."

"Very well, begin."

"Wait a minute, boss. You still have a few things to learn about hired labor. There are always certain working conditions and agreements involved, all of which I'll be happy to list for you."

CHAPTER EIGHT

"What I do not understand is why you must have the other slave?" Narsisi whined. "To have the woman of course is natural, as well as to have quarters of your own. My father has given his permission. But he also said that I and my brothers are to help you, that the secrets of the engine are to be revealed to no one else."

"Then trot right over to him and get permission for the slave Mikah to join me in the work. You can explain that he comes from the same land that I do, and that your secrets are mere children's toys to him. And if your dad wants any other reasons, tell him that I need skilled aid, someone who knows how to handle tools and who can be trusted to follow directions exactly as given. You and your brothers have entirely too many ideas of your own about how things should be done, and a tendency to leave details up to the gods, and have a good bash with the hammer if things don't work they way they should."

Narsisi retired, seething and muttering to himself, while Jason huddled over the oil stove planning the next step. It had taken most of the day to lay down logs for rollers and to push the sealed engine out into the sandy valley, far from the well site; open space was needed for any experiments in which a mistake could release a cloud of war gas. Even Edipon had finally seen the sense of this, though all of his tendencies were to conduct the experiments with great secretiveness, behind locked doors. He had granted permission only after skin walls had been erected to form an enclosure that could be guarded; it was only incidental that they acted as a much appreciated windbreak.

After a good deal of argument the dangling chains and shackles had been removed from Jason's arms and light-weight leg-irons substituted. He had to shuffle when he walked, but his arms were completely free; this was a great improvement over the chains, even though one of the brothers kept watch with a cocked crossbow as long as Jason wasn't fastened down. Now he had to get some tools and some idea of the technical knowledge of these people before he could proceed, which would necessarily entail one more battle over their precious secrets.

"Come on," he called to his guard, "let's find Edipon and give his ulcers another twinge."

After his first enthusiasm, the leader of the *d'zertanoj* was getting little pleasure out of his new project.

"You have quarters of your own," he grumbled to Jason, "and the slave woman to cook for you, and I have just given permission for the other slave to help you. Now more requests—do you want to drain all the blood from my body?"

"Let's not dramatize too much. I simply want some tools to get on with my work, and a look at your machine shop or wherever it is you do your mechanical work. I have to have some idea of the way you people solve mechanical problems before I can go to work on that box of tricks out there in the desert."

"Entrance is forbidden."

"Regulations are snapping like straws today, so we might as well go on and finish off a few more. Will you lead the way?"

The guards were reluctant to open the refinery building gates to Jason, and there were worried looks and much rattling of keys. A brace of elderly *d'zertanoj*, stinking of oil fumes, emerged from the interior and joined in a shouted argument with Edipon, whose will finally prevailed. Chained again, and guarded like a criminal, Jason was begrudgingly led into the dark interior, the contents of which were depressingly anticlimatic.

"Really primitive," Jason sneered, and he kicked at the boxful of clumsy hand-forged tools. The work was of the crudest, the product of a sort of neolithic machine age. The distilling retort had been laboriously formed from sheet copper and clumsily riveted together. It leaked mightily, as did the soldered seams on the hand-formed pipe. Most of the tools were blacksmith's tongs and hammers for heating and beating out shapes on the anvil. The only things that gladdened Jason's heart were the massive drill press and lathe that worked off the slave-power drive belts. In the tool holder of the lathe was clamped a chip of some hard mineral that did a good enough job of cutting the forged iron and low-carbon steel. Even more cheering was the screw-thread advance on the cutting head, which was used to produce the massive nuts and bolts that secured the *caro* wheels to their shafts.

It might have been worse. Jason sorted out the smallest and handiest tools and put them aside for his own use in the morning. The light was almost gone now and there would be no more work this day.

They left in armed procession, as they had come, and two guards showed him to the kennel-like room that was to be his private quarters. The heavy bolt thudded shut in the door behind him and he winced at the thick fumes of kerosene through which the light of the single-wick lamp barely penetrated.

Ijale crouched over the small oil stove cooking something in a pottery vessel. She looked up and smiled hesitatingly at Jason, then turned quickly back to the stove. Jason walked over, sniffed, and shuddered.

"What a feast! *Kreno* soup, and I suppose followed by fresh *kreno* and *kreno* salad. Tomorrow I'll see about getting a little variety into the diet."

"Ch'aka is great," she whispered without looking up. "Ch'aka is powerful . . ."

"Jason is the name, I lost the Ch'aka job when they took the uniform away."

". . . Jason is powerful to work charms on the *d'zertanoj* and make them do what he will. His slave thanks you."

He lifted her chin, and the dumb obedience in her eyes made him wince. "Can't we forget about the slavery bit? We are in this thing together and we'll get out of it together."

"We will escape, I know it. You will kill all the *d'zertanoj* and release your slaves and lead us home again where we can march and find *krenoj*, far from this terrible place."

"Some girls are sure easy to please. That is roughly what I had in mind, except when we get out of here we are going in the other direction, as far away from your *krenoj* crowd as I can get."

Ijale listened attentively, stirring the soup with one hand and scratching inside her leather wrappings with the other. Jason found himself scratching as well, and realized from the sore spots on his skin that he had been doing an awful lot of this since he had been dragged out of the ocean of this inhospitable planet.

"Enough is enough!" he exploded, and went over and

hammered on the door. "This place is a far cry from civilization as I know it, but that is no reason why we can't be as comfortable as possible." Chains and bolts rattled outside the door and Narsisi pushed his gloom-ridden face in.

"Why do you cry out? What is wrong?"

"I need some water, lots of it."

"But you have water," Narsisi said, puzzled, and pointed to a stone crock in the corner. "There is water there enough for days."

"By your standards, Nars old boy, not mine. I want at least ten times as much as that, and I want it now. And some soap, if there is such stuff in this barbaric place."

There was a good deal of argument involved, but Jason finally got his way by explaining that the water was needed for religious rites, to make sure that he would not fail in the work tomorrow. It came in a varied collection of containers, along with a shallow bowl full of powerful soft soap.

"We're in business," Jason chortled. "Take your clothes off—I have a surprise for you."

"Yes, Jason," Ijale said, smiling happily and lying down on her back.

"No! You're going to get a bath. Don't you know what a bath is?"

"No," she said, and shuddered. "It sounds evil."

"Over here, and off with the clothes," he ordered, poking at a hole in the floor. "This should serve as a drain—at least the water went away when I poured some into it."

The water was warmed on the stove, but Ijale still crouched against the wall and shuddered when he poured it over her. She screamed when he rubbed the slippery soap into her hair; however, he continued, with his hand over her mouth so that she wouldn't bring in the guards. He rubbed the soap into his own hair too, and his scalp tingled delightfully with the refreshing treatment. Some of the soap went in his ears, muffling them, so that the first intimation he had that the door was opened was the sound of Mikah's hoarse shout. He was standing in the doorway, finger pointed, and shaking with wrath, and Narsisi was standing behind him, peering over Mikah's shoulder with fascination at this weird religious rite.

"Degradation!" Mikah thundered. "You force this poor creature to bend to your will, humiliate her, strip her clothes

69

from her, and gaze upon her, though you are not united in lawful wedlock." He shielded his eyes from the sight with a raised arm. "You are evil, Jason, a demon of evil, and must be brought to justice—"

"*Out!*" Jason roared, and spun Mikah about and started him through the door with one of his practiced Ch'aka kicks. "The only evil here is in your mind, you snooping scut. I'm giving the girl the first scrubbing of her life, and you should be giving me a medal for bringing sanitation to the natives, instead of howling like that."

He pushed them both out the door and shouted at Narsisi : "I wanted this slave, but not *now*! Lock him up until morning, then bring him back." He slammed the door and made a mental note to get hold of a bolt to be placed on this side as well.

Ijale was shivering, and Jason rinsed off the suds with warm water and gave her a clean piece of fur to dry herself with. Her body, now that the dirt had been removed, looked young and strong, it was firm-breasted and wide-hipped— Then he recalled Mikah's accusations and, muttering angrily to himself, he turned away and stripped and scrubbed himself thoroughly, then used the last of the water to rinse out his clothes. The unaccustomed feeling of cleanliness raised his morale again, and he was humming as he blew out the lamp and finished drying himself in the darkness. He lay down and pulled up the sleeping furs, and was making plans for tackling the engine in the morning when Ijale's warm body pressed up against his, instantly driving away all thoughts of mechanical engineering.

"Here I am," she said, quite unnecessarily.

"Yes," he said, and coughed, for he was having some difficulty talking. "That's not really what I had in mind with the bath—"

"You are not too old. So what is wrong?" She sounded shocked.

"It's just that I don't want to take advantage, you must understand . . ." He was a little confused.

"What do you mean? You are one of *those* that doesn't like girls!" She started to cry and he could feel her body shaking.

"When in Rome—" he sighed, and patted her back.

There was more *krenoj* for breakfast, but Jason was

feeling too good physically to mind. He was scrubbed pink and clean, and the itching was gone even from his sprouting beard. The metalcloth of his Pyrran coverall had dried almost as soon as it had been washed, so he was wearing clean clothes as well. Ijale was still recovering from the traumatic effects of her bath, but she looked positively attractive with her skin cleaned and her hair washed and combed a bit. He would have to find some of the local cloth for her, for it would be a shame to ruin the good work by letting her get back into the badly cured skins she was used to wearing.

It was with a sensation of positive good feeling that he bellowed for the door to be opened and stamped through the cool morning to his place of labor. Mikah was already there, looking scruffy and angry as he rattled his chains. Jason gave him the friendliest of smiles, which only rubbed salt into the other's moral wounds.

"Leg-irons for him, too," Jason ordered. "And do it fast. We have a big job to do today." He turned back to the sealed engine, rubbing his hands together with anticipation.

The concealing hood was made of thin metal that could not hide many secrets. He carefully scratched away some of the paint and discovered a crimped and soldered joint where the sides met, but no other revealing marks. After some time spent tapping all over with his ear pressed to the metal, he was sure that the hood was just what he had thought it was when he first examined the thing : a double-walled metal container filled with liquid. Puncture it and you were dead. It was there merely to hide the secrets of the engine, and served no other function. Yet it had to be passed to service the steam engine—or did it? The construction was roughly cubical, and the hood covered only five sides. What about the sixth, the base?

"Now you're thinking, Jason," he said to himself, and knelt down to examine it. A wide flange, apparently of cast iron, projected all around, and was penetrated by four large bolt holes. The protective casing seemed to be soldered to the base, but there must be stronger concealed attachments, for it would not move even after he carefully scratched away some of the solder at the base. Therefore the answer had to be on the sixth side.

"Over here, Mikah," he called, and the man detached himself reluctantly from the warmth of the stove and shuffled up. "Come close and look at this medieval motive power while we talk, as if we are discussing business. Are you going to co-operate with me?"

"I do not want to, Jason. I am afraid that you will soil me with your touch, as you have others."

"Well, you're not so clean now—"

"I do not mean physically."

"Well, I do. You could certainly do with a bath and a good shampoo. I'm not worried about the state of your soul; you can battle that out on your own time. But if you will work with me I'll find a way to get us out of this place and to the city that made this engine, because if there is a way off this planet we'll find it only in the city."

"I know that, yet still I hesitate."

"Small sacrifices now for the greater good later. Isn't the entire purpose of this trip to get me back to justice? You're not going to accomplish that by rotting out the rest of your life as a slave."

"You are the devil's advocate the way you twist my conscience—but what you say is true. I will help you here so that we can escape."

"Fine. Now get to work. Take Narsisi and have him round up at least three good-sized poles, the kind we were chained to in the pumping gang. Bring them back here, along with a couple of shovels."

Slaves carried the poles only as far as the outside of the skin walls, for Edipon would not admit them inside, and it was up to Jason and Mikah to drag them laboriously to the site. The *d'zertanoj*, who never did physical labor, thought it very funny when Jason suggested that they help. Once the poles were in position by the engine, Jason dug channels beneath it and forced them under. When this was done he took turns with Mikah in digging out the sand beneath, until the engine stood over a pit, supported only by the poles. Jason let himself down and examined the bottom of the machine. It was smooth and featureless.

Once more he scratched away the paint with careful precision, until it was cleared around the edges. Here the solid metal gave way to solder and he picked at this until he discovered that a piece of sheet metal had been soldered at the edges and fastened to the bedplate. "Very tricky, these Appsalanoj," he said to himself, and attacked the solder with a knife blade. When one end was loose he slowly pulled the sheet of metal away, making sure that there was nothing attached to it, and that it had not been booby-trapped in any way. It came off easily enough and clanged down into the pit. The revealed surface was smooth hard metal.

"Enough for one day," Jason said, climbing out of the pit and brushing off his hands. It was now almost dark. "We've accomplished enough for now, and I want to think a bit before I go ahead. So far, luck has been on our side, but I don't think it should be this easy. I hope you brought your suitcase with you, Mikah, because you're moving in with me."

"Never! A sink of sin, depravity . . ."

Jason looked him coldly in the eye, and with each word he spoke he stabbed him in the chest with his finger to drive home the point : "You are moving in with me because that is essential to our plans. And if you'll stop referring to my moral weaknesses I'll stop talking about yours. Now come on."

Living with Mikah Samon was trying, but it was just barely possible. Mikah made Ijale and Jason go to the far wall and turn their backs and promise not to look while he bathed behind a screen of skins. They did so, but Jason exacted a small revenge by telling Ijale jokes so that they tittered together and Mikah would be sure they were laughing at him. The screen of skins remained after the bath, and was reinforced, and Mikah retired behind it to sleep.

The following morning, under the frightened gaze of his guards, Jason tackled the underside of the baseplate. He had been thinking about it a good part of the night, and he put his theories to the test at once. By pressing hard on a knife he could make a good groove in the metal. It was not as soft as the solder, but seemed to be some simple alloy containing a good percentage of lead. What could it be concealing? Probing carefully with the point of the knife, he covered the bottom in a regular pattern. The depth of the metal was uniform except in two spots where he found irregularities; they were on the midline of the rectangular base, and equidistant from the ends and sides. Picking and scraping, he uncovered two familiar-looking shapes, each as big as his head.

"Mikah, get down in this hole and look at these things. Tell me what you think they are."

Mikah scratched his beard and prodded with his finger. "They're still covered with this metal. I can't be sure . . ."

"I'm not asking you to be sure of anything—just tell me what they make you think of."

"Why—big nuts, of course. Threaded on the ends of bolts. But they are so big. . . ."

"They would have to be if they hold the entire metal case on. I think we are getting very close now to the mystery of how to open the engine—and this is the time to be careful. I still can't believe it is as easy as this to crack the secret. I'm going to whittle a wooden template of the nut, then have a wrench made. While I'm gone you stay down here and pick all the metal off the bolt and out of the screw threads. We can think this thing through for a while, but sooner or later I'm going to have to take a stab at turning one of those nuts. And I find it very hard to forget about that mustard gas."

Making the wrench put a small strain on the local technology, and all of the old men who enjoyed the title of Masters of the Still went into consultation over it. One of them was a fair blacksmith, and after a ritual sacrifice and a round of prayers he shoved a bar of iron into the charcoal and Jason pumped the bellows until it glowed white hot. With much hammering and cursing, it was laboriously formed into a sturdy open-end wrench with an offset head to get at the countersunk nuts. Jason made sure that the opening was slightly undersized, then took the untempered wrench to the work site and filed the jaws to an exact fit. After being reheated and quenched in oil he had the tool that he hoped would do the job.

Edipon must have been keeping track of the work progress, for he was waiting near the engine when Jason returned with the completed wrench.

"I have been under," he announced, "and have seen the nuts that the devilish Appsalanoj have concealed within solid metal. Who would have suspected! It still seems to me impossible that one metal could be hidden within another. How could that be done?"

"Easy enough. The base of the assembled engine was put into a form and the molten covering metal poured into it. It must have a much lower melting point than the steel of the engine, so there would be no damage. They just have a better knowledge of metal technology in the city, and counted upon your ignorance."

"Ignorance! You insult—"

"I take it back. I just meant they thought they could get away with the trick; and since they didn't, they are the stupid ones. Does that satisfy you?"

"What do you do next?"

"I take off the nuts and when I do there is a good chance that the poison-hood will be released and can simply be lifted off."

"It is too dangerous for you to do. The fiends may have other traps ready when the nut is turned. I will send a strong slave to turn them while we watch from a distance. His death will not matter."

"I'm touched by your concern for my health, but as much as I would like to take advantage of the offer, I cannot. I've been over the same ground and reached the reluctant conclusion that this is one job of work that I have to do myself. Taking off those nuts looks entirely too easy, and that's what makes me suspicious. I'm going to do it and look out for any more trickery at the same time—and that is something that only I can do. Now I suggest you withdraw with the troops to a safer spot."

There was no hesitation about leaving; footsteps rustled quickly on the sand and Jason was alone. The leather walls flapped slackly in the wind, and there was no other sound. Jason spat on his palms, controlled a slight shiver, and slid into the pit. The wrench fitted neatly over the nut, he wrapped both hands around it, and, bracing his leg against the pit wall, began to pull.

And stopped. Three turns of thread on the bolt projected below the nut, scraped clean of metal by the industrious Mikah. Something about them looked very wrong, though he didn't know quite what. But suspicion was enough.

"Mikah," he shouted, but had to call loudly two more times before his assistant poked his head tentatively around the screen. "Nip over to the petroleum works and get me one of their bolts threaded with a nut—any size, it doesn't matter."

Jason warmed his hands by the stove until Mikah returned with the oily bolt, then waved him out to rejoin the others. Back in the pit, he held it up next to the protruding section of Appsalan bolt and almost shouted with joy. The threads on the engine bolt were canted at a slightly different angle : where one ran up, the other ran down. The Appsalan threads had been cut in reverse, with a lefthand thread.

Throughout the galaxy there existed as many technical and cultural differences as there were planets, but one of the few things they all had in common, inherited from their terrestrial ancestors, was a uniformity of thread. Jason had never thought about it before, but when he mentally ran through his experiences on different planets he realized that they were all the same. Screws went into wood, bolts went into threaded holes, and nuts all went onto bolts when you turned them with a clockwise motion. Counterclockwise removed them. In his hand was the crude *d'zertano* nut and bolt, and when he tried it it moved in the same manner. But the engine bolt did not : it had to be turned clockwise to *remove* it.

Dropping the nut and bolt, he placed the wrench on the massive engine bolt and slowly applied pressure in what felt like the completely wrong direction—as if he were tightening, not loosening. It gave slowly, first a quarter-turn, then a half-turn. Bit by bit the projecting threads vanished, until they were level with the surface of the nut. It turned easily now, and within a minute it fell into the pit. He threw the wrench after it and scrambled out. Standing at the edge, he carefully sniffed the air, ready to run at the slightest smell of gas. There was nothing.

The second nut came off as easily as the first, and with no ill effects. Jason pushed a sharp chisel between the upper case and the baseplate where he had removed the solder, and when he leaned on it the case shifted slightly, held down only by its own weight.

From the entrance to the enclosure he shouted to the group huddled in the distance. "Come on back—this job is almost finished."

They all took turns at sliding into the pit and looking at the projecting bolts, and made appreciative sounds when Jason leaned on the chisel and showed that the case was free.

"There is still the little matter of taking it off," he told them, "and I'm sure that grabbing and heaving is the wrong way. That was my first idea, but the people who assembled that thing had some bad trouble in store for anyone who tightened those nuts instead of loosening them. Until we find out what that is, we are going to tread very lightly. Do you have any big blocks of ice around here, Edipon? It is winter now, isn't it?"

"Ice? Winter?" Edipon mumbled, caught off guard by the change of subject. He rubbed at the reddened tip of his prominent nose. "Of course it is winter. Ice—there must be ice on the higher lakes in the mountain; they are always frozen at this time of the year. But what do you want ice for?"

"You get it and I'll show you. Have it cut in nice flat blocks that I can stack. I'm not going to lift off the hood— I'm going to drop the engine out from underneath it!"

By the time the slaves had brought the ice down from the distant lakes Jason had rigged a strong wooden frame flat on the ground around the engine and pushed sharpened metal wedges under the hood; then he had secured the wedges to the frame. Now, if the engine was lowered into the pit, the hood would stay above, supported by the wedges. The ice would take care of this. Jason built a foundation of ice under the engine and then slipped out the supporting bars. As the ice melted, the engine would be gently lowered into the pit.

The weather remained cold, and the ice refused to melt until Jason had the pit ringed with smoking oil stoves. Water began to run down into the pit and Mikah went to work bailing it out, while the gap between the hood and the baseplate widened. The melting continued for the rest of the day and almost all of the night. Red-eyed and exhausted, Jason and Mikah supervised the soggy sinking, and when the *d'zertanoj* returned at dawn the engine rested in a pool of mud on the bottom of the pit : the hood was off.

"They're tricky devils over there in Appsala, but Jason dinAlt wasn't born yesterday," he exulted. "Do you see that crock sitting there on top of the engine?" He pointed to a sealed container of thick glass, the size of a small barrel, filled with an oily greenish liquid; it was clamped down tightly with padded supports. "That's the booby-trap. The nuts I took off were on the threaded ends of two bars that held the hood on, but instead of being fastened directly to the hood they were connected by a crossbar that rested on top of that jug. If either nut was tightened instead of being loosened the bar would have bent and broken the glass. I'll give you exactly one guess as to what would have happened then."

"The poison liquid!"

"None other. And the double-walled hood is filled with it too. I suggest that as soon as we have dug a deep hole in the desert the hood and container be buried and forgotten about. I doubt if the engine has many other surprises in store, but I'll be careful as I work on it."

"You can fix it? You know what is wrong with it?" Edipon was trembling with joy.

"Not yet. I have barely looked at the thing. In fact, one look was enough to convince that the job will be as easy as stealing *krenoj* from a blind man. The engine is as inefficient and clumsy in construction as your petroleum still. If you people put one tenth of the energy into research and improving your product as you do into hiding it from the competition, you would all be flying jets."

"I forgive your insult because you have done us a service. You will now fix this engine and the other engines. A new day is breaking for us!"

Jason yawned. "Right now it is a new night that is breaking for me. I have sleep to make up. See if you can talk your sons into wiping the water off that engine before it rusts away, and when I get back I'll see what I can do about getting it into running condition."

CHAPTER NINE

Edipon's good mood continued and Jason took advantage of it by extracting as many concessions as possible. By hinting that there might be more traps in the engine, he easily gained permission to do all the work on the original site instead of inside the sealed and guarded buildings. A covered shed gave them protection from the weather, and a test stand was constructed to hold the engines when Jason worked on them. This was of a unique design and was built to Jason's exacting specifications; and since no one, including Mikah, had ever heard of or seen a test stand before, Jason, had his way.

The first engine proved to have a burnt-out bearing and Jason rebuilt it by melting down the original bearing metal and casting it in position. When he unbolted the head of the massive single cylinder he shuddered at the clearance around the piston; he could fit his fingers into the opening between the piston and the cylinder wall. By introducing cylinder rings, he doubled the compression and power output. When Edipon saw the turn of speed the rebuilt engine gave his *caro*, he hugged Jason to his bosom and promised him the highest reward. This turned out to be a small piece of meat every day to relieve the monotony of the *kreno* meals, and a doubled guard to make sure that his valuable property did not escape. Their food up to now had consisted only of *krenoj*, and Jason shuddered while he admitted that he was actually growing used to them.

Jason had his own plans and kept busy manufacturing a number of pieces of equipment that had nothing at all to do with his engine-overhauling business. While these were being assembled he went about lining up a little aid.

"What would you do if I gave you a club?" he asked a burly slave whom he was helping to haul a log towards his workshop. Narsisi and one of his brothers lazed out of earshot, bored by the routine of the guard duty.

"What I do with club?" the slave grunted, forehead furrowing and mouth gaping with the effort of thought.

"That's what I asked. And keep pulling while you think. I don't want the guards to notice anything."

"If I have club, I kill!" the slave announced excitedly, fingers grasping eagerly for coveted weapon.

"Would you kill me?"

"I have club, I kill you, you not so big."

"But if I gave you the club, wouldn't I be your friend? Then wouldn't you want to kill someone else?"

The novelty of this alien thought stopped the slave dead, and he scratched his head perplexedly until Narsisi lashed him back to work. Jason sighed and found another slave to try his sales program on.

It took a while, but the idea was eventually percolating through the ranks of the slaves. All they had to look forward to from the *d'zertanoj* was back-breaking labor and an early death. Jason offered them something else—weapons, a chance to kill their masters, and even more killing later when they marched on Appsala. It was difficult for them to grasp the idea that they must work together to accomplish this, and not kill Jason and each other as soon as they received weapons. It was a chancy plan at best, and would probably break down long before any visit could be made to the city. But the revolt should be enough to free them from bondage, even if the slaves fled afterwards. There were less than fifty *d'zertanoj* at this well station, all men, with their women and children at some other settlement further back in the hills. It would not be too hard to kill them or chase them off, and long before they could bring reinforcements Jason and his runaway slaves would be gone. There was just one factor missing from his plans, and a new draft of slaves solved even that problem for him.

"Happy days," he laughed, pushing open the door to his quarters and rubbing his hands together with glee. The guard shoved Mikah in after him and locked the door. Jason secured it with his own interior bolt, then waved the two others over to the corner furthest from the door and the tiny window opening.

"New slaves today," he told them, "and one of them is from Appsala, a mercenary or a soldier that they captured on a skirmish. He knows that they will never let him live long enough to leave here, so he was grateful for any suggestions I had."

"This is man's talk I do not understand," Ijale said, turning away and starting towards the cooking fire.

"You'll understand this," Jason said, taking her by the shoulder. "The soldier knows where Appsala is and can lead us there. The time has come to think about leaving this place."

He had all of Ijale's attention now, and Mikah's as well. "How is this?" she gasped.

"I have been making my plans. I have enough files and lockpicks now to crack into every room in this place, a few weapons, the key to the armory, and every able-bodied slave on my side."

"What do you plan to do?" Mikah asked.

"Stage a slave revolt in the best style. The slaves fight the *d'zertanoj* and we get away, perhaps with an army helping us, but at least we get away."

"You are talking *revolution*!" Mikah bellowed, and Jason jumped him and knocked him to the floor. Ijale held his legs down while Jason squatted on his chest and covered his mouth.

"What is the matter with you? Do you want to spend the rest of your life rebuilding engines? They are guarding us too well for there to be much chance of our breaking out on our own, so we need allies. We have them ready made—all the slaves."

"Brevilushun," Mikah mumbled through the restraining fingers.

"Of course it's a revolution. It is also the only possible chance of survival that these poor devils will ever have. Now they are human cattle, beaten and killed on whim. You can't be feeling sorry for the *d'zertanoj*—every one of them is a murderer ten times over. You've seen them beat people to death. Do you feel they are too nice to suffer a revolution?"

Mikah relaxed and Jason moved his hand slightly, ready to clamp down if the other's voice rose above a whisper.

"Of course they are not nice," Mikah said. "They are beasts in human garb. I feel no mercy for them, and they should be wiped out and blotted from the face of the earth, as were Sodom and Gomorrah. But it cannot be done by revolution : revolution is evil, inherently evil."

Jason stifled a groan. "Try telling that to two-thirds of the governments that now exist, since that's how many were founded—by revolution. Nice, liberal, democratic governments—that were started by a bunch of lads with guns and the immense desire to run things in a manner more beneficial to themselves. How else do you get rid of the powers on your neck if there is no way to vote them away legally? If you can't vote them—shoot them."

"Bloody revolution, it cannot be!"

"All right, no revolution," Jason said, getting up and wiping his hands in disgust. "We'll change the name. How about calling it a prison break? No, you wouldn't like that either. I have it—liberation! We are going to strike the chains off these poor people and restore them to the lands from which they were stolen. The little fact that the slave-holders regard them as property and won't think much of the idea, and therefore might get hurt in the process, shouldn't bother you. So—will you join me in this liberation movement?"

"It is still revolution."

"It is whatever I decide to call it!" Jason raged. "You come along with me on the plans, or you will be left behind when we go. You have my word on that." He went over and helped himself to some soup and waited for his anger to simmer down.

"I cannot do it . . . I cannot do it," Mikah brooded, staring into his rapidly cooling soup as into an oracular crystal ball, seeking guidance there. Jason turned his back on him.

"Don't end up like him," he warned Ijale, pointing his spoon back over his shoulder. "Not that there is much chance that you ever will, coming as you do from a society with its feet firmly planted on the ground, or on the grave, to be more accurate. Your people see only concrete facts, and only the most obvious ones, and as simple an abstraction as 'trust' seems beyond you. While this long-faced clown can only think in abstractions of abstractions, and the more unreal they are the better. I bet he even worries about how many angels can dance on the head of a pin."

"I do not worry about that," Mikah broke in, over-hearing the remark. "But I do think about it once in a while. It is a problem that cannot be lightly dismissed."

"You see?"

Ijale nodded. "If he is wrong, and I am wrong—then you must be the only one who is right." She nodded in satisfaction at the thought.

"Very nice of you to say so." Jason smiled. "And true

82

too. I lay no claims to infallibility, but I am damn sure that I can see the difference between abstractions and facts a lot better than either of you, and I am certainly more adroit at handling them." He reached his hand over his shoulder and patted himself on the back. "The Jason dinAlt fan-club meeting is now adjourned.

"Monster of arrogance!" Mikah exclaimed.

"Oh, keep still."

"Pride goeth before a fall! You are a maledicent and idolatrous antipietist . . ."

"Very good."

". . . and I grieve that I could have considered, for even a second, aiding you or standing by while you sin, and I fear for the weakness of my own soul that I have not been able to resist temptation as I should. It grieves me, but I must do my duty." He banged loudly on the door and called, "Guard! Guard!"

Jason dropped his bowl and started to scramble to his feet, but slipped in the spilled soup and fell. As he stood up again, the locks rattled on the door, and it opened. If he could reach Mikah before the idiot opened his mouth he would close it forever, or at least knock him out before it was too late.

But it was already too late. Narsisi poked his head in and blinked sleepily; Mikah struck his most dramatic pose and pointed to Jason. "Seize and arrest that man. I denounce him for attempted revolution, for planning red murder!"

Jason skidded to a halt and back-tracked, diving into a bag of his personal belongings that lay against the wall. He scrabbled in it, then kicked the contents about, and finally came up with a metal-forming hammer that had a weighty solid lead head.

"More traitor you," Jason shouted at Mikah, and he ran at Narsisi, who had been dumbly watching the performance and mulling over Mikah's words. Slow as he appeared to be, there was nothing wrong with his reflexes, and his shield snapped up and took Jason's blow, while his club spun over neatly and rapped Jason on the back of the hand: the numbed fingers opened and the hammer dropped to the floor.

"I think you two better come with me; my father will know what to do," Narsisi said, pushing Jason and Mikah ahead of him out of the door. He locked it and called for one of his brothers to stand guard, then prodded his captives down the hall. They shuffled along in their leg-irons, Mikah nobly as a martyr and Jason seething and grinding his teeth.

Edipon was not at all stupid when it came to slave rebellions, and he sized up the situation even faster than Narsisi could relate it.

"I have been expecting this, so it comes as no surprise." His eyes held a mean glitter when he leveled them at Jason. "I knew the time would come when you would try to overthrow me, which was why I permitted this other one to assist you and to learn your skills. As I expected, he has betrayed you to gain your position, which I award him now."

"Betray? I did this for no personal gain," Mikah protested.

"Only the purest of motives." Jason laughed coldly. "Don't believe a word this pious crook tells you, Edipon. I'm not planning any revolution—he said that just to get my job."

"You calumniate me, Jason! I never lie—you are planning revolt. You told me—"

"Silence, both of you! Or I'll have both of you beaten to death. This is my judgment. The slave Mikah has betrayed the slave Jason, and whether the slave Jason is planning rebellion or not is completely unimportant. His assistant would not have denounced him unless he was sure that he could do the work as well, which is the only fact that has any importance to me. Your ideas about a worker class have troubled me, Jason, and I will be glad to kill them and you at the same time. Chain him with the slaves. Mikah, I award you Jason's quarters and his woman, and as long as you do the work well I will not kill you. Do it a long time and you will live a long time."

"Only the purest of motives—is that what you said, Mikah?" Jason shouted back as he was kicked from the room.

The descent from the pinnacle of power was swift. Within half an hour new shackles were on Jason's wrist and he was chained to the wall in a dark room filled with other slaves. His leg-irons had been left on as an additional reminder of his new status. As soon as the door was closed he rattled the chains and examined them in the dim light of a distant lamp.

"How comes the revolution?" the slave chained next to him leaned over and asked in a hoarse whisper.

"Very funny, ha-ha," was Jason's answer, and then he moved closer for a better look at the man, who had a fine case of strabismus, his eyes pointing in independent directions. "You look familiar—are you the new slave I talked to today?"

"That's me, Snarbi, fine soldier, pikeman, checked out on club and dagger, seven kills and two possibles on my record. You can check it yourself at the guildhall."

"I remember it all, Snarbi, including the fact that you know your way back to Appsala."

"I been around."

"Then the revolution is still on; in fact, it is starting right now, but I want to keep it small. Instead of freeing all these slaves, what do you say to the idea that we two escape by ourselves?"

"Best idea I've heard since torture was invented. We don't need all these stupid types, they just get in the way. Keep the operation small and fast, that's what I always say."

"I always say that too," Jason agreed, digging into his boot with his fingertip. He had managed to shove his best file and a lockpick into hiding there while Mikah was betraying him back in their room. The attack on Narsisi with the hammer had just been a cover-up.

Jason had made the file himself after many attempts at manufacturing and hardening steel, and the experiments had been successful. He picked out the clay that covered the cut he had made in his leg-cuffs and tackled the soft iron with vigor; within three minutes they were lying on the floor.

"You are a magician?" Snarbi whispered.

"Mechanic. On this planet they're the same thing." He looked around, but the exhausted slaves were all asleep and had heard nothing. Wrapping a piece of leather around the file to muffle the sound, he began to file a link in the chain that secured the shackles on his wrists. "Snarbi," he said quietly, "are we on the same chain?"

"Yeah, the chain goes through these iron cuff things and

holds the whole row of slaves together. The other end goes out through a hole in the wall."

"Couldn't be better. I'm filing one of these links, and when it goes we're both free. See if you can't slip the chain through the holes in your shackles and lay it down without letting the next slave know what is happening. We'll wear the iron cuffs for now. There is no time to play around with them, and they shouldn't bother us too much. Do the guards come through here at all during the night to check on the slaves?"

"Not since I been here. They just wake us up in the morning by pulling the chain."

"Then let's hope that's what happens tonight, because we are going to need plenty of time. *There!*" The file had cut through the link. "See if you can get enough of a grip on the other end of this link while I hold this end, and we'll try to bend it open a bit."

They strained silently until the opening gaped wide enough and the link fell through. They slipped the chain and laid it silently on the ground, then moved noiselessly to the door.

"Is there a guard outside?" Jason asked.

"Not that I know. I don't think they have enough men here to guard all the slaves."

The door would not budge when they pushed against it, and there was just light enough to make out the large key-hole of a massive inset lock. Jason probed lightly with the pick, and curled his lip in contempt.

"These idiots have left the key in the lock." He pulled off the stiffest of his leather wrappings, and after flattening it out pushed it under the badly fitting bottom edge of the door, leaving just a bit to hold on to. Then through the key-hole he poked lightly at the key and heard it thud to the ground outside. When he pulled the leather back, the key was lying in the center of it. The door unlocked silently and a moment later they were outside, staring tensely into the darkness.

"Let's go! Run, get away from here," Snarbi said, but Jason grabbed him by the throat and pulled him back.

"Isn't there one bit of intelligence on this planet? How are you going to get to Appsala without food or water—and if you find some, how can you carry enough? If you want to stay alive, follow instructions. I'm going to lock

86

this door first so that no one stumbles onto our escape by accident. Then we are going to get some transport and leave here in style. Agreed?"

The answer was only a choked rattle until Jason opened his fingers a bit and let some air into the man's lungs. A labored groan must have meant assent, for Snarbi tottered after Jason when he made his way through the dark alleys between the buildings.

Getting clear of the walled refinery town presented no problem, since the few sentries were looking for trouble only from the outside. It was equally easy to approach Jason's leather-walled worksite from the rear and slip through at the spot where Jason had cut the leather and sewn up the opening with thin twin.

"Sit here and touch nothing, or you will be cursed for life," he commanded the shivering Snarbi; then he slipped toward the front entrance with a small sledge hammer clutched in his fist. He was pleased to see one of Edipon's other sons on guard duty, leaning against a pole, dozing. Jason gently lifted his leather helmet with his free hand and tapped once with the hammer : the guard slept even more soundly.

"Now we can get to work," Jason said when he went back inside. He clicked a firelighter to the wick of a lantern.

"What are you doing?" Snarbi asked, terrified. "They'll see us, kill us—escaped slaves. . . ."

"Stick with me, Snarbi, and you'll be wearing shoes. Lights here can't be seen by the sentries—I made sure of that when I chose the site. And we have a piece of work to do before we leave—we have to build a *caro*."

They did not have to build it from scratch, but there was enough truth in the statement to justify it. His most recently rebuilt and most powerful engine was still bolted to the test stand, a fact that justified all the night's risks. Three *caro* wheels lay among the other debris of the camp, and two of them had to be bolted to the engine while it was still on the stand. The ends of the driving axle cleared the edges of the stand, and Jason threaded the securing wheel bolts into place and utilized Snarbi to tighten them. At the other end of the stand was a strong, swiveling post that had been a support for his test instruments, and seemed strangely large for this purpose. It was. When the instruments were stripped away, a single bar remained, projecting backwards like a tiller handle. When a third wheel was fitted with a stub axle and slid into place in the forked lower end of the post, the test stand looked remarkably like a three-wheeled, steerable, steam-engine-powered platform that was mounted on legs. That is exactly what it was, what Jason had designed it to be from the first, and the supporting legs came away with the same ease with which the other parts had been attached. Eventual escape had always taken first priority in his plans.

Snarbi dragged over the crockery jars of oil, water, and fuel while Jason filled the tanks. He started the fire under the boiler and loaded aboard tools and the small supply of *krenoj* he had managed to set aside from their rations. All of this took time; it would soon be dawn and they would have to leave before then, and he could no longer avoid making up his mind.

He could not leave Ijale here, and if he went to get her he could not refuse to take Mikah as well. The man had saved his life, no matter what murderous idiocies he had managed to pull since then. Jason believed that you owed something to a man who prolonged your existence, but he also wondered just how much he still owed. In Mikah's case, he felt the balance of the debt to be mighty small, if not overdrawn. Perhaps this one last time . . .

"Keep an eye on the engine—I'll be back as soon as I can," he said, jumping to the ground and putting on his equipment.

"You want me to do *what?* Stay here with this devil machine? I cannot! It will burn and consume me."

"Act your age, Snarbi, your physical age if not your mental one. This rolling junk pile was made by men and repaired and improved by me—no demons involved. It burns oil to make heat that makes steam that goes to this tube to push that rod to make those wheels go around so we can move, and that is as much of theory of the steam engine as you are going to get from me. Maybe you can understand this better—I, only I, can get you safely away from here. Therefore you will stay and do as I say, or I will beat your brains in. Clear?"

Snarbi nodded dumbly.

"Fine. All you have to do is sit here and look at this little green disk—see it? If it should pop out before I come back, turn *this* handle in *this* direction. Is that clear? That way, the safety valve won't blow and wake the whole country, and we'll still have a head of steam."

Jason went out past the still silent sentry and headed back towards the refinery station. Instead of a club or a dagger, he was armed with a well-tempered broadsword that he had managed to manufacture under the noses of the guards. They had examined everything he brought from the worksite, since he had been working in the evenings in his room, but they ignored everything he manufactured as being beyond their comprehension. This primordial mental attitude had been of immense value, for in addition to the sword he carried a sack of molotails, a simple weapon of assault whose origin was lost in pre-history. Small crocks were filled with the most combustible of the refinery's fractions and were wrapped around with cloth that he had soaked in the same liquid. The stench made him dizzy, and he hoped that they would repay his efforts when the time came. He could only hope, for they were completely untried. In use, one lit the outer covering and threw them. The crockery burst on impact and the fuse ignited the contents. Theoretically.

Getting back in proved to be as easy as getting out, and Jason felt a twinge of regret. His subconscious had obviously been hoping that there would be a disturbance and he would have to retreat to save himself—his subconscious obviously being very short on interest in saving the slave girl and his nemesis, particularly at the risk of his own skin. But he was back in the building where his quarters were, and was trying to peer around the corner to see if a guard was at the door. There was, and he seemed to be dozing, but something jerked him awake. He had heard nothing, but he sniffed the air and wrinkled his nose; the powerful smell of water-of-power from Jason's molotails had roused him and he spotted Jason before the latter could pull back.

"Who is there?" the guard shouted, and he advanced at a lumbering run.

There was no quiet way out of this, and Jason leaped out with an echoing shout and lunged. The blade went right under the man's guard—it must have been that he had never seen a sword before—and the tip caught him full in the throat. He expired with a bubbling wail that stirred voices deeper in the building. Jason sprang over the corpse and tore at the multifold bolts and locks that sealed the door. Footsteps were running in the distance when he finally threw the door open and ran in.

"Get out, and quick, we're escaping!" he shouted at them and pushed the dazed Ijale towards the door. He took a great deal of pleasure in landing a tremendous kick that literally lifted Mikah through the opening, where he collided with Edipon, who had just run up waving a club. Jason leaped over the tumbled forms, rapped Edipon behind the ear with the hilt of his sword, and dragged Mikah to his feet.

"Get out to the engine works," he ordered his still uncomprehending companions. "I have a *caro* there that we can get away in." They finally broke into clumsy motion.

Shouts sounded behind him and an armed mob of *d'zertanoj* ran into view. Jason pulled down the hall light, burning his hand on the hot base as he did so, and applied its open flame to one of his molotails. The wick caught with a burst of flame and he threw it at approaching soldiers before it could burn his hand more seriously. It flew towards them, hit the wall, and broke; inflammable fuel spurted in every direction but the flame went out.

Jason cursed, and grappled for another molotail, for if they didn't work he was dead. The *d'zertanoj* had hesitated a moment rather than walk through the puddle of spilled water-of-power, and in that instant he hurled the second fire bomb. This one burst nicely too, and lived up to its maker's expectations when it ignited the first molotail as well, and the passageway filled with a curtain of fire. Holding his hand around the lamp flame so it wouldn't go out, Jason ran after the others.

As yet, the alarm had not spread outside the building. Jason bolted the door from the outside; by the time this was broken open and the confusion sorted out they would be clear of the buildings. There was no need for the lamp now and it would only give him away, so he blew it out. From the desert came a continuous ear-piercing scream.

"He's done it," Jason groaned. "That's the safety valve on the steam engine!"

He bumped into Ijale and Mikah, who were milling about confusedly in the dark, kicked Mikah again out of sheer hatred of all mankind, and led them towards the worksite at a dead run.

They escaped unharmed, mainly because of the confusion on all sides of them. The *d'zertanoj* seemed to have never experienced a night attack before, which they apparently thought this was, and they did an incredible amount of rushing about and shouting. The burning building and the unconscious form of Edipon that was carried from the blaze made the general excitement and disorder even worse. All the *d'zertanoj* had been roused by the scream of the safety valve, which was still bleeding irreplaceable steam into the night air.

In the confusion, the fleeing slaves were not noticed, and Jason led them around the guard post on the walls and directly towards the worksite. They were spotted as they crossed the empty ground, and after some hesitation the guard ran in pursuit. Jason was leading the enemy directly to his precious steam wagon, but he had no choice. In any case, the thing was making its presence known, and unless he reached it at once the head of steam would be gone and they would be trapped. He leaped the recumbent guard at the entrance and ran towards his machine. Snarbi was cowering behind one wheel, but there was no time to give him any attention. As Jason jumped onto the platform the safety valve closed, and the sullen stillness was frightening.

Frantically he spun valves and shot a glance at the indicator : there wasn't enough steam left to roll ten meters. Water gurgled and the boiler hissed and clacked at him, while cries of anger came from the *d'zertanoj* as they ran into the enclosure and saw the bootleg *caro*. Jason thrust the end of a molotail into the firebox; it caught fire and he turned and hurled it at them. The angry cries turned into screams of fear as the tongues of flame licked up at the pursuers, and they retreated in disorder. Jason ran after them and hastened their departure with another molotail. They seemed to be retreating as far as the refinery walls, but he could not be sure in the darkness whether some of them weren't creeping around to the sides.

He hurried back to the *caro*, tapped on the unmoving pressure indicator, and opened the fuel feed wide. As an afterthought he wired down the safety valve, since his reinforced boiler should hold more pressure than the valve had been originally adjusted for. Once this was finished, he could only wait, for there was nothing else that could be done until the pressure built up again. The *d'zertanoj* would rally, someone would take charge, and they would attack the worksite. If enough pressure built up before this happened, they could escape. If not . . .

"Mikah—and you too, you cowering slob Snarbi, get behind this thing and push," Jason said.

"What has happened?" Mikah asked. "Have you started the revolution? If so, I will give no aid . . ."

"We're escaping, if that's all right with you. Just I, Ijale, and a guide to show us the way. You don't have to come."

"I will join you. There is nothing criminal in escaping from these barbarians."

"It's very nice of you to say so. Now push. I want this steammobile in the center, far from the walls, and pointing towards the desert. Down the valley, I guess—is that right, Snarbi?"

"Down the valley, sure, that's the way." His voice was still rasping from the earlier throttling, Jason was pleased to notice.

"Stop it here, and everyone aboard. Grab on to those bars I've bolted along the sides so you won't get bounced off— if we ever start moving, that is."

Jason took a quick look through his workshop to make sure everything they might need was already loaded, then reluctantly he climbed aboard. He blew out the lantern and they sat there in the darkness while the tension mounted, their faces lit from below by the flickering glow from the firebox. There was no way to measure time; each second seemed to take an eternity to drag by. The walls of the worksite cut off any view of the outside, and within a few moments imagination had peopled the night with silent creeping hordes, huddling about the thin barrier of leather, ready to swoop down and crush them in an instant.

"Let's run for it," Snarbi gurgled, and he tried to jump from the platform. "We're trapped here, we'll never get away."

Jason tripped him and knocked him flat, then pounded his head against the floor planks a few times until he quieted.

"I can sympathize with that poor man," Mikah said severely. "You are a brute, Jason, to punish him for his natural feelings. Cease your sadistic attack and join me in a prayer."

"If this poor man you are so sorry for had done his duty

and watched the boiler, we would all be safely away from here by now. And if you have enough breath for a prayer, put it to better use by blowing into the firebox. It's not going to be wishes, prayers, or divine intervention that gets us out of here—it's a head of steam . . ."

A howled battle cry was echoed by massed voices, and a squad of *d'zertanoj* burst through the entrance. At the same instant the rear of the leather wall went down and more armed men swarmed over it. The immobile *caro* was trapped between the two groups of attackers, who laughed in glee as they charged. Jason, cursing, lit four molotails at the same time and hurled them, two and two, in opposite directions. Before they hit, he had jumped to the steam valve and wound it open; with a hissing clank the *caro* shuddered and got under way. For the moment the attackers were held back by the walls of flame, and they screamed as the machine moved away at right angles from between their two groups. The air whistled with crossbow bolts, but most were badly aimed and only a few thudded into the baggage.

With each revolution of the wheels their speed picked up, and when they hit the walls the hides parted with a creaking snap. Strips of leather whipped at them, then they were through. The shouts grew fainter and the fires grew dimmer behind them as they streaked down the valley at a suicidal pace, hissing and rattling over the bumps. Jason clung to the tiller and shouted for Mikah to come relieve him. For if he let go of the thing they would turn and crash in an instant, and as long as he held it he couldn't cut down the steam. Some of this finally got through to Mikah and he crawled forward, grasping desperately at every handhold, until he crouched beside Jason.

"Grab the tiller and hold it straight, and steer around anything big enough to see."

As soon as the steering was taken over, Jason worked his way back to the engine and throttled down; they slowed to a clanking walk, then stopped completely. Ijale moaned, and Jason felt as if every inch of his body had been beaten with hammers. There was no sign of pursuit; it would be at least an hour before they could raise steam in the *caroj*, and no one on foot could possibly have matched their own headlong pace. The lantern he had used earlier had vanished during the wild ride, so Jason dug out another one of his own construction.

"On your feet, Snarbi," he ordered. "I've cracked us all out of slavery, and now it is time for you to do some of the guiding that you were telling me about. I never did have a chance to build headlights for this machine, so you will have to walk ahead with this light and pick out a nice smooth track going in the right direction."

Snarbi climbed down unsteadily and walked out in front of them. Jason opened the valve a bit and they clattered forward on his trail as Mikah turned the tiller to follow. Ijale crawled over and settled herself against Jason's side, shivering with cold and fright. He patted her shoulder.

"Relax," he said. "From now on this is just a pleasure trip."

CHAPTER TEN

They were six days out of Putl'ko and their supplies were almost exhausted. The country, once they were away from the mountains, became more fertile, and undulating pampas of grass with enough streams and herds of beasts to assure that they did not starve. It was fuel that mattered, and that afternoon Jason had opened their last jar. They stopped a few hours before dark, for their fresh meat was gone, and Snarbi took the crossbow and went out to shoot something for the pot. Since he was the only one who could handle the clumsy weapon with any kind of skill, in spite of his ocular deficiences, and who knew about the local game, this task had been assigned to him. With longer contact, his fear of the *caro* had lessened, and his self-esteem rose with his ability as a hunter recognized. He strolled arrogantly out into the knee-high grass, crossbow over his shoulder, whistling tunelessly through his teeth. Jason stared after him and once again felt a growing unease.

"I don't trust that wall-eyed mercenary. I don't trust him for one second," he muttered.

"Were you talking to me?" Mikah asked.

"I wasn't, but I might as well now. Have you noticed anything interesting about the country we have been passing through, anything different?"

"Nothing. It is a wilderness, untouched by the hand of man."

"Then you must be blind, because I have been seeing things the last two days, and I know just as little about woodcraft as you do. Ijale," he called, and she looked up from the boiler over which she was heating a thin stew of their last *krenoj*. "Leave that stuff—it tastes just as bad whatever is done to it, and if Snarbi has any luck we'll be having roast meat. Tell me, have you seen anything strange or different about the land we passed through today?"

"Nothing strange, just signs of people. Twice we passed places where grass was flat and branches broken, as if a *caro* passed two or three days ago, maybe more. And once there was a place where someone had built a cooking fire, but that was very old."

"Nothing to be seen, Mikah?" Jason said, with raised eyebrows. "See what a lifetime of *kreno* hunting can do for the sense of observation and terrain."

"I am no savage. You cannot expect me to look out for that sort of thing."

"I don't. I have learned to expect very little from you besides trouble. Only now I am going to need your help. This is Snabi's last night of freedom, whether he knows it or not, and I don't want him standing guard tonight, so you and I will split the shift."

Mikah was astonished. "I do not understand. What do you mean when you say this is his last night of freedom?"

"It should be obvious by now, even to you, after seeing how the social ethic works on this planet. What did you think we were going to do when we came to Appsala—follow Snarbi like sheep to the slaughter? I have no idea what he is planning; I just know he must be planning something. When I ask him about the city he only answers in generalities. Of course he is a hired mercenary who wouldn't know too much of the details, but he must know a lot more than he is telling us. He says we are still four days away from the city. My guess is that we are no more than one or two. In the morning I intend to grab him and tie him up, then swing over to those hills there and find a place to hole up. I'll fix some chains for Snarbi so he can't get away, and then I'll do a scout of the city."

"You are going to chain this poor man, make a slave of him for no reason!"

"I'm not going to make a slave of him, I'm just going to chain him to make sure he doesn't lead us into some trap that will benefit him. This souped-up *caro* is valuable enough to tempt any of the locals, and if he can sell me as an engine-mechanic slave his fortune is made."

"I will not hear this!" Mikah stormed. "You condemn the man on no evidence at all, just because of your mean-minded suspicions. Judge not lest ye be judged yourself! And play the hypocrite as well, because I well remember your telling me that a man is innocent until proven guilty."

"Well, this man is guilty, if you want to put it that way, guilty of being a member of this broken-down society, which means that he will always act in certain ways at certain times. Haven't you learned anything about these people yet? ... Ijale!" She looked up from her contented munching on a *kreno*, obviously not listening to the argument. "Tell me, what is your opinion? We are coming soon to a place where Snarbi has friends, or people who will help him. What do you think he will do?"

"Say hello to the people he knows? Maybe they will give him a *kreno*." She smiled in satisfaction at her answer, and took another bite.

"That's not quite what I had in mind," Jason said patiently. "What if we three are with him when we come to the people, and the people see us and the *caro* . . ."

She sat up, alarmed. "We can't go with him! If he has people there they will fight us, make us slaves, take the *caro*. You must kill Snarbi at once."

"Bloodthirsty heathen . . ." Mikah began in his best denunciatory voice, but he stopped when he saw Jason pick up a heavy hammer.

"Don't you understand yet?" Jason asked. "By tying up Snarbi, I'm only conforming to a local code of ethics, like saluting in the army, or not eating with your fingers in polite society. In fact, I'm being a little slipshod, since by local custom I really should kill him before he can make trouble for us."

"It cannot be. I cannot believe it. You cannot judge and condemn a man upon such flimsy evidence."

"I'm not condemning him," Jason said with growing irritation. "I'm just making sure that he can't cause us any trouble. You don't have to agree with me to help me; just don't get in my way. And split the guard with me tonight. Whatever I do in the morning will be on my shoulders and no concern of yours."

"He is returning," Ijale whispered, and a moment later Snarbi came through the high grass.

"Got a *cervo*," he announced proudly, and dropped the animal down before them. "Cut him up, makes good chops and roast. We eat tonight."

He seemed completely innocent and without guile; the only thing that appeared guilty about him was his shifty gaze, which could be blamed on his crossed eyes. Jason wondered for a second if his assessment of the danger was correct; then thought of where he was and lost his doubts. Snarbi would be committing no crime if he tried to kill or enslave them; he would just be doing what any ordinary slave-holding barbarian would do in his place. Jason searched through his toolbox for some rivets that could be used to fasten the leg-irons on the man.

They had a filling dinner and the others turned in at dusk and were quickly asleep. Jason, tired from the labors of the trip and heavy with food, forced himself to remain awake, trying to keep alert for trouble, both from within the camp and from without. When he became too sleepy, he paced around the camp until the cold drove him back to the shelter of the still warm boiler. Above him, the stars wheeled slowly, and when one bright one reached the zenith he estimated it was midnight, or a bit after. He shook Mikah awake.

"You're on now. Keep your eyes and ears open for anything stirring, and don't forget a careful watch there." He jerked him thumb at Snarbi's silent form. "Wake me up at once if there is anything suspicious."

Sleep came instantly, and Jason barely stirred until the first light of dawn touched the sky. Only the brightest stars were visible, and he could see a ground fog rising from the grass around them. Near him were the huddled forms of the two sleepers; the further one shifted in his sleep and Jason realized it was Mikah.

He bounded out of his skin covers and grabbed the other man by the shoulders. "What are you doing asleep?" he raged. "You were supposed to be on guard!"

Mikah opened his eyes and blinked with majestic assurance. "I was on guard, but towards morning Snarbi awoke and offered to take his turn. I could not refuse him."

"You couldn't *what*? After what I said—"

"That was why. I could not judge an innocent man guilty and be a party to your unfair action. Therefore I left him on guard."

"*You left him on guard!*" The words almost choked Jason, "Then where is he?" Do you see anyone on guard?"

Mikah looked around in a careful circle and saw that there were only the two of them and the wakening Ijale. "He seems to have gone. He has proved his untrustworthiness, and in the future we will not allow him to stand guard."

Jason drew his foot back for a kick, then realized he had no time for such indulgences and dived for the steamobile. The firemaker worked at the first try for a change, and he lit the boiler. It roared merrily, but when he tapped the indicator he saw that the fuel was almost gone. There should be enough left in the last jug to take them to safety before whatever trouble Snarbi was planning arrived—but the jug was gone.

"That tears it," Jason said bitterly after a hectic search of the *caro* and the surrounding plain. The water-of-power had vanished with Snarbi, who, afraid as he was of the steam engine, apparently knew enough from observing Jason fueling the thing to realize that it could not move without the vital liquid.

An empty feeling of resignation had replaced Jason's first rage : he should have known better than to trust Mikah with anything, particularly when it involved an ethical point. He stared at the man, now calmly eating a bit of cold roast, and marveled at his unruffled calm.

"This doesn't bother you," he said, "the fact that you have condemned us all to slavery again ?"

"I did what was right. I had no other choice. We must live as moral creatures, or sink to the level of the animals."

"But when you live with people who behave like animals —how do you survive ?"

"You live as they do—as you do, Jason," he said with jestic judgment, "twisting and turning with fear, but unable to avoid your fate no matter how you squirm. Or you live as I have done, as a man of conviction, knowing what is right and not letting your head be turned by the petty needs of the day. And if one lives this way, one can die happy."

"Then die happy !" Jason snarled, and he reached for his sword, but he settled back again glumly without picking it up. "To think that I ever thought I could teach you anything about the reality of existence here, when you have never experienced reality before, nor ever will until the day you die. You carry your own attitudes, which are your reality, around with you all the time, and they are more solid to you than this ground we are sitting on."

"For once we are in agreement, Jason. I have tried to open your eyes to the true light, but you turn away and will not see. You ignore the Eternal Law for the exigencies of the moment, and are therefore damned."

The pressure indicator on the boiler hissed and popped out, but the fuel level was at the absolute bottom.

"Grab some food for breakfast, Ijale," Jason said, "and

get away from this machine. The fuel is gone and it's finished."

"I shall make a bundle to carry, and we will escape on foot."

"No, that's out of the question. Snarbi knows this country, and he knew we would find out at dawn that he was missing. Whatever kind of trouble he is bringing is already on the way, and we wouldn't be able to escape on foot. So we might as well save our energy. But they aren't getting my hand-made, super-charged steamobile!" he added with sudden vehemence, snatching up the crossbow. "Back, both of you, far back. They'll make a slave of me for my talents, but no free samples go with it. If they want one of these hot-rod steam wagons they are going to have to pay for it!"

Jason lay down flat at the maximum range of the crossbow and his third quarrel hit the boiler. It went up with a most satisfactory bang and small pieces of metal and wood rained down all around. In the distance he heard shouting and the barking of dogs.

When he stood up he could see a distant line of men advancing through the tall grass, and when they were closer large dogs were also visible, tugging at their leashes. Though they must have come far in a few hours, they approached at a steady trot—experienced runners in thin leather garments, each carrying a short laminated bow and a full quiver of arrows. They swooped up in a semicircle, their great hounds slavering to be loosed, and stopped when the three strangers were within bow range. They notched their arrows and waited, alert, staying well clear of the smoking ruins of the *caro* until Snarbi finally staggered up, half supported by two other runners.

"You now belong to . . . the Hertug Persson . . . and are his slaves . . ." Snarbi said. He seemed too exhausted to notice his surroundings. "What happened to the *caro*?" He screamed this last when he spotted the smoking wreck, and would have collapsed except for the sustaining arms. Evidently the new slaves decreased in value with the loss of the machine.

Snarbi stumbled over to it and, when none of the soldiers would help him, gathered up what he could find of Jason's artifacts and tools. When he had bundled them up, and the foot cavalry saw that he suffered no harm from the contact, they reluctantly agreed to carry them. One of the soldiers, identical in dress with the others, seemed to be in charge, and when he signaled a return they closed in on the three prisoners and nudged them to their feet with drawn bows.

"I'm coming, I'm coming," Jason said, gnawing on a bone, "but I'm going to finish my breakfast first. I see an endless vista of *krenoj* stretching before me, and I intend to enjoy this last meal before entering servitude."

The lead soldiers looked confused and turned to their officer for orders. "Who is this?" he asked Snarbi, pointing at the still seated Jason. "Is there any reason why I should not kill him?"

"You can't!" Snarbi choked, and turned a dirty shade of white. "He is the one who built the devil-wagon and knows all of its secrets. Hertug Persson will torture him to build another."

Jason wiped his fingers on the grass and stood up. "All right, gentlemen, let's go. And on the way perhaps someone can tell me just who Hertug Persson is and what is going to happen next."

"I'll tell you," Snarbi bragged as they started the march. "He is Hertug of the Perssonoj. I have fought for the Perssonoj and they knew me, and I saw the Hertug himself and he believed me. The Personnoj are very powerful in Appsala and have many powerful secrets, but they are not as powerful as the Trozelligoj, who have the secrets of the *caroj* and the *jetilo*. I knew I could ask any price of the Perssonoj if I brought them the secret of the *caroj*. And I will." He thrust his face close to Jason's with a fierce grimace. "You will tell them the secret. I will help them torture you until you tell."

Jason put out his toe as they walked and Snarbi tripped over it, and when the traitor fell he walked the length of his body. None of the soldiers paid any attention to this incident. When they had passed Snarbi staggered to his feet and tottered after them, shouting curses. Jason hardly heard them, for he had troubles enough as it was.

CHAPTER ELEVEN

Seen from the surrounding hills, Appsala looked like a burning city that was being washed into the sea. Only when they had come closer was it clear that the smoke was from the multifold chimneys, both large and small, that studded the buildings, and that the city began at the shore and covered a number of islands in what must be a shallow lagoon. Large seagoing ships were tied up at the seaward side of the city, and closer to the mainland smaller craft were being poled through the canals. Jason searched anxiously for a spaceport or any signs of interstellar culture, but saw nothing. Then the hills intervened as the trail cut to one side and approached the sea some distance from the city.

A fair-sized sailing vessel was tied up at the end of a stone wharf, obviously awaiting them, and the captives were tied hand and foot and tossed into the hold. Jason managed to wriggle around until he could get his eye to a crack between two badly fitting planks, and he gave a running travelog of the short cruise, apparently for the edification of his companions, but really for his own benefit, since the sound of his own voice always cheered him and gave him courage.

"Our voyage is nearing its close, and before us opens up the romantic and ancient city of Appsala, famed for its loathsome customs, murderous natives, and archaic sanitation facilities, of which the watery channel this ship is now entering seems to be the major cloaca. There are islands on both sides, the smaller ones covered with hovels so decrepit that in comparison the holes in the grounds of the humblest animals are as palaces, while the larger islands seem to be forts, each one walled and barbicaned, and presenting a warlike face to the world. There couldn't be that many forts in a town this size, so I am led to believe that each one is undoubtedly the guarded stronghold of one of the tribes, groups, or clans that our friend Judas told us about. Look on these monuments to ultimate selfishness and beware: this is the end product of the system that begins with slave-holders like the former Ch'aka with their tribes of *kreno* crackers, and builds up through familial hierachies like the *d'zertanoj*, and reaches its zenith of depravity behind those strong walls. It is still absolute power that rules absolutely, each man out for all that he can get, the only way to climb being over the bodies of others, and all physical discoveries and inventions being treated as private and personal secrets to be hidden and used only for personal gain. Never have I seen human greed and selfishness carried to such extremes, and I admire Homo sapiens' capacity to follow through on an idea, no matter how it hurts."

The ship lost way as it backed its sails, and Jason fell from his precarious perch into the stinking bilge. "The descent of man," he muttered, and inched his way out.

Piles grated along the sides, and with much shouting and cursed orders the ship came to a halt. The hatch above was slid back and the three captives were rushed to the deck. The ship was tied up to a dock in a pool of water surrounded by buildings and high walls. Behind them a large sea gate was just swinging shut, through which the ship had entered from the canal. They could see no more because they were pushed into a doorway and through halls and past guards until they ended up in a large central room. It was unfurnished except for the dais at the far end on which stood a large rusty iron throne. The man on the throne, undoubtedly the Hertug Persson, sported a magnificent white beard and shoulder-length hair; his nose was round and red, his eyes blue and watery. He nibbled at a *kreno* impaled delicately on a two-tined iron fork.

"Tell me," the Hertug shouted suddenly, "why you should not be killed at once?"

"We are your slaves, Hertug, we are your slaves," everyone in the room shouted in unison, at the same time waving their hands in the air. Jason missed the first chorus, but came in on the second. Only Mikah did not join in the chant-and-wave, speaking instead in a solitary voice after the pledge of allegiance was completed.

"I am no man's slave."

The commander of the soldiers swung his thick bow in a short arc that terminated on the top of Mikah's head : he dropped stunned to the floor.

"You have a new slave, oh Hertug," the commander said.

"Which is the one who knows the secrets of the *caroj*?" the Hertug asked, and Snarbi pointed at Jason.

"Him there, oh Mightiness. He can make *caroj* and he can make the monster that burns and moves them. I know because I watched him do it. He also made balls of fire that burned the *d'zertanoj*, and many other things. I brought him to be your slave so that he could make *caroj* for the Perssonoj. Here are the pieces of the *caro* we traveled in, that were left after it was consumed by its own fire." Snarbi shook the tools and burnt fragments out onto the floor, and the Hertug curled his lip at them.

"What proof is this?" he asked, and turned to Jason. "These things mean nothing. How can you prove to me, slave, that you can do the things he says?"

Jason entertained briefly the idea of denying all knowledge of the matter, which would be a neat revenge against Snarbi, who would certainly meet a sticky end for causing all this trouble for nothing, but he discarded the thought as quickly as it had come. Partly for humanitarian reasons, for Snarbi could not help being what he was, but mostly because Jason had no particular desire to be put to the torture. He knew nothing about the local torture methods, and he wanted to keep it that way.

"Proof is easy, Hertug of all the Perssonoj, because I know everything about everything. I can build machines that walk, that talk, that run, fly, swim, bark like a dog, and roll on their backs."

"You will build a *caro* for me?"

"It could be arranged, if you have the right kind of tools for me to use. But I must first know what is the specialty of your clan, if you know what I mean. For instance, the Trozelligoj make motors, and the *d'zertanoj* pump oil : what do your people do?"

"You cannot know as much as you say if you do not know of the glories of the Perssonoj!"

"I come from a distant land and, as you know, news travels slowly around these parts."

"Not around the Perssonoj," the Hertug said scornfully, and he thumped his chest. "We can talk across the width of the country, and always know where our enemies are. We can send magic to make light in a glass ball, or magic that will pluck the sword from an enemy's hand and drive terror into his heart."

"It sounds as if your gang has the monopoly on electricity,

104

which is good to hear. If you have some heavy forging equipment—"

"Stop!" the Hertug interrupted. "Leave! Out—everyone except the *sciuloj*. Not the new slave, he stays here," he shouted when the soldiers seized Jason.

When the others had left, only a handful of men remained who were all a little long in the tooth. Each wore a brazen, sunburst-type decoration on his chest. They were undoubtedly adept in the secret electrical arts, and they fingered their weapons and grumbled with unconcealed anger at Jason's forbidden knowledge.

The Hertug spoke to him again. "You used a sacred word. Who told it to you? Speak quickly, or you will be killed."

"Didn't I tell you I knew everything? I can build a *caro* and, given a little time, I can improve on your electrical works, if your technology is on the same level as the rest of this planet."

"Do you know what lies behind the forbidden portal?" the Hertug asked, pointing to a barred, locked, and guarded door at the other end of the room. "There is no way you can have seen what is there, but if you can tell me what lies beyond it I will know you are the wizard that you claim you are."

"I have a very strange feeling that I have been over this ground once before," Jason sighed. "All right, here goes. You people here make electricity, maybe chemically, though I doubt if you would get enough power that way, so you must have a generator of some sort. That will be a big magnet, a piece of special iron that can pick up other iron, and you spin wire around fast next to it, and out comes electricity. You pipe this through copper wire to whatever devices you have—and they can't be many. You say you talk across the country. I'll bet you don't talk at all, but send little clicks—I'm right, am I not?" The foot shuffling and the rising buzz from the adepts were sure signs that he was hitting close.

"I have an idea for you : I think I'll invent the telephone. Instead of the old clickety-clack, how would you like to *really* talk across the country? Speak into a gadget here, and have your voice come out at the far end of the wire?"

The Hertug's piggy little eyes blinked greedily. "It is said that in the old days this could be done, but we have tried and have failed. Can you do this thing?"

"I can—if we can come to an agreement first. But before I make any promises I have to see your equipment."

This brought mutters of complaint about secrecy, but in the end avarice won over taboo and the door to the holy of holies was opened for Jason while two of the *sciuloj*, with bared daggers ready, stood at his sides. The Hertug led the way, followed by Jason and his septuagenarian bodyguard, with the rest of the *sciuloj* tottering after. Each of them bowed and mumbled a prayer as he crossed the sacred threshold, while it was all Jason could do to keep himself from breaking into contemptuous laughter.

A rotating shaft—undoubtedly slave-powered—entered the large chamber through the far wall and turned a ramshackle collection of belts and pulleys that eventually hooked up to a crude and ugly machine that rattled and squeaked and shook the floor under their feet. At first sight it baffled Jason, until he examined its components and realized what it was.

"What else should I have expected?" he said to himself. "If there are two ways of doing anything, leave it to these people to use the worst one."

The final, cartwheel-sized pulley was fixed to a wooden shaft that rotated at an impressive speed, except when one of the belts jumped out of place, which was something that occurred with monotonous regularity. This happened while Jason was watching, and the shaft instantly slowed so that he could see that iron rings studded with smaller U-shaped pieces of iron, were fixed all along its length. These were half hidden inside a birdcage of looped wires that was suspended about the shaft. The whole thing looked like an illustration from a bronze age edition of *First Steps in Electricity*.

"Does not your soul cringe in awe before these wonders?" Hertug asked, noticing Jason's dropped jaw and glassy eye.

"It cringes all right," Jason told him. "But only in pain from that ill-conceived collection of mechanical misconceptions."

"Blasphemer!" the Hertug shrieked. "Slay him!"

"Wait a minute!" Jason said, holding tight to the dagger arms of the two nearest *sciuloj* and interposing their bodies between his body and the others' blades. "Don't misunderstand. That's a great generator you have there, a seventh wonder of the world—though most of the wonder is how it manages to produce any electricity. A tremendous invention, years ahead of its time. However, I might be able to suggest a few minor modifications that would produce more electricity with less work. I suppose that you are aware that an electric current is generated in a wire when a magnetic field is moved across it?"

"I do not intend to discuss theology with a non-believer," the Hertug said coldly.

"Theology or science, call it what you will, the answers still come out the same." Jason twisted a bit with his Pyrran-hardened muscles and the two old men squealed and dropped their daggers to the floor. The rest of the *sciuloj* seemed reluctant to press the attack. "But did you ever stop to think that you could get an electrical current just as easily by moving the *wire* through the magnetic field, instead of the other way around? You can get the same current flow that way with about a tenth of the work."

"We have always done it this way, and what was good enough for our ancestors—"

"I know, I know, don't finish the quote. I seem to have heard it before on this planet." The armed *sciuloj* began to close in on him again, their daggers ready. "Look, Hertug —do you want me slain or not? Let your boys know."

"Slay him not," the Hertug said after a moment's thought. "What he says may be true. He may be able to assist us in the operation of our holy machines."

With the threat removed for the moment, Jason examined the large, ungainly apparatus that filled the far end of the room, this time making some attempt to control his horrified reactions. "I suppose that yon sacred wonder is your holy telegraph?"

"None other," the Hertug said reverently. Jason shuddered.

Copper wires came down from the ceiling above and terminated in a clumsily wound electromagnet positioned close to the flat iron shaft of a pendulum. When a current surged through the electromagnet it would attract the shaft; and when the current was turned off, the weight on the end of the pendulum would drag it back to somewhere near the vertical. A sharp metal scriber was fixed to the bottom of the weight, and the point of the scriber was dug into the wax coating of a long strip of copper. This strip ran in grooves so that it moved at right angles to the pendulum's swing, dragged forward by a weight-powered system of meshed wooden gears.

While Jason watched, the rattling mechanism jerked into motion. The electromagnet buzzed, the pendulum jerked, the needle drew an incision across the wax, and gears squeaked, and the cord fastened to a hole in the end of the strip began to draw it forwards. Attentive *sciuloj* stood ready to put another wax-coated strip into position when the first one was finished.

Close by, completed message strips were being made legible by pouring red liquid over them. This ran off the waxen surface but was trapped by the needle-scratched grooves. A shaky red line appeared running the length of the strips, with V-shaped extensions wherever the scribing needle had been deflected. These were carried to a long table where the coded information was copied off onto slates. Everything considered, it was a slow, clumsy, inept method of transmitting information. Jason rubbed his hands together.

"Oh, Hertug of all the Perssonoj," he intoned, "I have looked on your holy wonders and stand in awe, indeed I do. Far be it for a mere mortal to improve on the works of the gods, at least not right now, but it is within my power to pass on to you certain other secrets of electricity that the gods have imparted to me."

"Such as what?" the Hertug asked, eyes slitted.

"Such as the—let's see, what is the Esperanto word for it —such as the *akumulatoro*. Do you know of this?"

"The word is mentioned in some of the older holy writings, but that is all we know of it." The Hertug was licking his lips.

"Then get ready to add a new chapter, because I'm going to provide you with a Leyden jar, free and gratis, along with complete instructions on how to make more. This is a way of putting electricity in a bottle, just as if it were water. Then later we can go on to more sophisticated batteries."

"If you can do this thing you shall be suitably rewarded. Fail, and you will be . . ."

"No threats, Hertug; we've gone far beyond that stage. And no rewards either. I told you this was a free sample with no strings attached—perhaps just a few physical comforts for me while I'm working : the fetters struck off, a supply of *krenoj* and water, and such like. Then, if you like what I've done and want more, we can make a deal. Agreed?"

"I will consider your requests," the Hertug said.

"A simple yes or no will do. What can you possibly lose in an arrangement like this?"

"Your companions will be held prisoners to be slain instantly if you transgress."

"A fine idea. And if you want to get some work out of the one called Mikah—like hard labor, for instance—that is perfectly agreeable. I'll need some special materials that I don't see here. A wide-mouthed jar and a good supply of tin."

"Tin? I know it not."

"Yes, you do. It's the white metal you mix with copper to make your bronze."

"*Stano*. We have a goodly supply."

"Have them bring it around and I'll get to work."

In theory a Leyden jar is simple enough to manufacture —if all the materials are on hand. Getting the correct materials was Jason's biggest problem. The Perssonoj did no glass blowing themselves, but bought everything they needed from the Vitristoj clan, who labored at their secret furnaces. These glass blowers produced a few stock-sized bottles, buttons, drinking glasses, knobbly plate glass, and half a dozen other items. None of their bottles could be adapted to this use, and they were horrified at Jason's suggestion that they produce a new bottle to his specifications. The offer of hard cash drained away most of their dismay, and after studying Jason's clay models they reluctantly agreed to produce a similar bottle for a staggering sum. The Hertug grumbled mightily, but finally he paid over the required number of stamped and punctured gold coins strung on a wire.

"Your death will be horrible," he told Jason, "if your *akumulatoro* fails."

"Have faith, and all will be well," Jason reassured him, and he returned to browbeating the metal workers, who suffered as they tried to hammer sheet tin into thin foil.

Jason had seen neither Mikah nor Ijale since they had all been dragged into the Perssonoj stronghold, but he did not worry about them. Ijale was well adapted to the slave life, so she would get into no trouble while he was selling the Hertug on the wonders of his electrical knowledge. Mikah, however, was not used to being a slave, and Jason cherished the hope that this would lead to bad trouble, resulting in physical contusions. After the last fiasco, his reservoir of good will for the man had drained dry.

"It has arrived," the Hertug announced, and he and all the *sciuloj* stood around mumbling suspiciously while the wrappings were removed from the glass jar.

"Not too bad," Jason said, holding it up to the light to see how thick the sides were. "Except that this is the large twenty-liter economy size—about four times as big as the model I sent them."

"For a large price a large jar," the Hertug said. "That is only right. Why do you complain? Do you fear failure?"

"I fear nothing. It's just a lot more trouble to build a model this size. It can also be dangerous; these Leyden jars can take quite a charge."

Inoring the onlookers, Jason coated the jar inside and out with his lumpy tinfoil, stopping about two-thirds of the way up from the bottom. He then whittled a plug from *gumi*, a rubber-like material that had good insulating qualities, and drilled a hole through it. The Perssonoj watched, mystified, as he pushed an iron rod through this hole, then attached a short iron chain to the longer end, and fixed a round iron ball to the shorter.

"Finished," he announced.

"But—what does it do?" the Hertug asked, puzzled.

"I demonstrate." Jason pushed the plug into the wide mouth of the jar so that the chain rested on the inner lining of tinfoil. He pointed to the ball that projected from the top. "This is attached to the negative pole of your generator; electricity flows through the rod and chain and is collected on the tin lining. We run the generator until the jar is full, then disconnect the input. The jar will then hold an electrical charge that we can draw off by hooking up to the ball. Understand?"

"Madness!" one of the older *sciuloj* cackled, and averted the infection of insanity by rotating his forefinger next to his temple.

"Wait and see," Jason said, with a calmness he did not feel. He had built the Leyden jar from a dim memory of a textbook illustration studied in his youth, and there was no guarantee the thing would work. He grounded the positive pole of the generator, then did the same with the outer coating of the jar by running a wire from it to a spike driven down through a cracked floor tile into the damp soil below.

"Let her roll!" he shouted and stepped back, arms folded.

The generator groaned and rotated, but nothing visible happened. He let it go for several minutes, since he had no idea of its output or of the jar's capacity, and a lot depended on the results of this first experiment. Finally the sneering asides of the *sciuloj* grew louder, so he stepped forward and disconnected the jar with a flip of a dry stick.

"Stop the generator; the work is done. The *akumulatoro* is filled brimful with the holy force of electricity." He pulled over the demonstration unit he had prepared, a row of the crude incandescent light bulbs wired in series. There ought to be enough of a charge in the Leyden jar to overcome the weak resistance of the carbon filaments and light them up. He hoped.

"Blasphemy!" screeched the same elderly *sciulo*, shuffling forward. "It is sacred writ that the holy force can only flow when the road is complete, and when the road of flow is broken no force shall move. Yet this outlander dares tell us that holiness now resides in this jar to which but one wire was connected. Lies and blasphemy!"

"I wouldn't do that if I were you . . ." Jason suggested to the oldster, who was now pointing to the ball on top of the Leyden jar.

"There is no force here—there can be no force here. . . ." His voice broke off suddenly as he waved his finger an inch from the ball. A fat blue spark snapped between his fingertip and the charged metal, and the *sciulo* screamed hoarsely and dropped to the floor. One of his fellows knelt to examine him, then turned his frightened gaze to the jar.

"He is dead," he breathed.

"You can't say I didn't warn him," Jason said, then decided to press hard while luck with on his side. "It was *he* who blasphemed!" Jason shouted, and the old men cringed away. "The holy force was stored in the jar, and he doubted and the force struck him dead. Doubt no more, or you will all meet the same fate! Our work as *sciuloj*," he added, giving himself a promotion from slavery, "is to harness the powers of electricity for the greater glory of the Hertug. Let this be a reminder, lest we ever forget." They eyed the body, shuffled backwards, and got the idea very clearly.

"The holy force can kill," the Hertug said, smiling down

at the corpse and dry-washing his hands. "This is indeed wonderful news. I always knew it could give shocks and cause burns, but never knew it held this great power. Our enemies will shrink before us."

"Without a doubt," Jason said, striking while the iron was hot, and whipping out the drawings he had carefully prepared. "Take a look at these other wonders. An electrical motor to lift and pull things, a light called the carbon arc that can pierce the night, a way of coating things with a thin layer of metal, and many more. You can have them all, Hertug."

"Begin construction at once!"

"Instantly—as soon as we agree on the terms of my contract."

"I don't like the sound of that."

"You'll like it even less when you hear the details, but it will be well worth it." He bent forward and whispered in the Hertug's ear. "How would you like a machine that could blow down the walls of your enemies' fortresses so that you could defeat them and capture their secrets?"

"Clear the room," the Hertug commanded, and when they were alone he turned his shrewd little red eyes on Jason. "What is this contract you mentioned?"

"Freedom for me, a position as your personal adviser, slaves, jewels, girls, good food—all the usual things that go with the job. In return I will build for you all of the devices I have mentioned, and a good many more. There is nothing I cannot do! And all of this will be yours . . ."

"I will destroy them all—I will rule Appsala!"

"That's sort of what I had in mind. And the better things are for you, the better they will be for me. I ask no more than a comfortable life and the chance to work on my inventions, being a man of small ambition. I'll be happy puttering about in the lab—while you will rule the world."

"You ask much . . ."

"I'll supply much. I'll tell you what—take a day or two to make up your mind, while I produce one more invention for your instruction and edification."

Jason remembered the spark that had struck down the old man, and it gave him fresh hope. It might be the way off this planet.

CHAPTER TWELVE

"When will this be completed?" the Hertug asked, poking at the parts spread over Jason's workbench.

"Tomorrow morning, though I work all night, oh Hertug. But even before it is finished I have another gift for you, a way to improve your telegraph system."

"It needs no improvement! It is as it was in our forefathers' day, and—"

"I'm not going to change anything; forefathers always know best, I agree. I'll just give you a new operating technique. Look at this—" and he held out one of the metal strips with the scribed wax coating. "Can you read the message?"

"Of course, but it takes great powers of concentration, for it is a deep mystery."

"Not that deep; in one look I divined all its horrible simplicity."

"You blaspheme!"

"Not really. Look here: that's a *B*, isn't it—two jiggles from the magic pendulum?"

The Hertug counted on his fingers. "It is a *B*, you are correct. But how can you tell?"

Jason concealed his scorn. "It was hard to figure out, but all things are as an open book to me. *B* is the second letter in the alphabet, so it is coded by two strokes. *C* is three— still easy; but you end up with *z*, needing twenty-six bashes at the sending key, which is just a nonsensical waste of time. When all you have to do is modify your equipment slightly in order to send two different signals—let's be original and call one a 'dot' and the other a 'dash'. Now, using these two signals, a short and a long impulse, we can transcribe every letter of the alphabet in a maximum of four increments. Understand?"

"There is a buzzing in my head, and it is difficult to follow ..."

"Sleep on it. In the morning my invention will be finished, and at that time I will demonstrate my code."

The Hertug left, muttering to himself, and Jason finished the last windings on the armature for his new generator.

"What do you call it?" the Hertug asked, walking around the tall, ornate wooden box.

"This is an All Hail the Hertug Maker, a new source of worship, respect, and finance for Your Excellency. It is to be placed in the temple, or your local equivalent, where the public will pay for the privilege of doing you homage. Observe : I am a loyal subject who enters the temple. I give a donation to the priest and grasp this handle that projects from the side, and turn." He began cranking lustily and the sound of turning gears and growing whine came from the cabinet. "Now watch the top."

Projecting from the upper surface of the cabinet were two curved metal arms that ended in copper spheres separated by an air space. The Hertug gasped and recoiled as a blue spark snapped across the gap.

"That will impress the peasants, won't it?" Jason said. "Now—observe the sparks and notice their sequence. First three short sparks, then three long ones, then three short ones again."

He stopped cranking and handed the Hertug a clearly inscribed sheet of vellum, a doctored version of the standard interstellar code. "Notice. Three dots stand for *H* and three dashes signify *A*. Therefore as long as this handle is turned the machine sends out *H.A.H.* in code, signifying *Huraoj al Hertug*, All Hail the Hertug ! An impressive device that will keep the priests busy and out of mischief and your local followers entertained. While at the same time it will cry your praises with the voice of electricity, over and over, night and day."

The Hertug turned the handle and watched the sparks with glowing eyes. "It shall be unveiled in the temple tomorrow. But there are sacred designs that must be inscribed on it first. Perhaps some gold ..."

"Jewels too, the richer-looking the better. People aren't going to pay to work a holy hand-organ unless it looks impressive."

Jason listened happily as the sparks crackled out. They might be saying *H.A.H.* in the local code, but it would be S.O.S. to an off-worlder. And any spaceship with a decent receiver that entered the atmosphere of this planet should pick up the broad-spectrum radio waves from the spark gap. There might even be one hearing the message now, turning the loop of the direction finder, zeroing in on the signal.

If he only had a receiver he could hear their answering message, but it didn't matter, for shortly he would hear the roar of their rockets as they dropped on Appsala. . . .

Nothing happened. Jason had sent out the first S.O.S. over twelve hours earlier, but now he reluctantly abandoned any hope of immediate rescue. The best thing to do now was to get established soundly and comfortably while he waited for a ship to arrive. He did not let himself dwell on the possibility that a spacer might not approach this backwater planet during his lifetime.

"I have been considering your requests," the Hertug said, turning away from the spark-gap transmitter. "You might have a small apartment of your own, perhaps a slave or two, enough food to satisfy, and on holy days wine and beer. . . ."

"Nothing stronger?"

"You cannot obtain anything stronger; the Perssonoj wines from our fields on the slopes of Mount Malvigla are well known for their potency."

"They'll be even better known once I run them through a still. I can see a number of small improvements that will have to be made if I am to stay around here for any length of time. I may even have to invent the water closet before I get rheumatism from the drafts in your primitive jakes. There is a lot to be done. What we will have to do first is draw up a list of priorities, at the top of which will be money. Some of the things I plan to build for your greater glory will be a little expensive, so it would be best if we allowed for that by filling the treasury beforehand. I suppose you have no religious principles that forbid you getting richer?"

"None," the Hertug answered, very positively.

"Then we can let it rest there for now. With Your Excellency's permission, I shall repair to my new quarters and get some sleep, after which I shall prepare a list of projects for your edification and selection."

"That is satisfactory to me. And do not forget the things to make money."

"Top of the list."

Though Jason had the liberty of the sealed and holy workrooms, he had four bodyguard jailers who stayed very close to him the rest of the time, treading on his heels and breathing *kreno* fumes down the back of his neck.

"Do you know where my new quarters are?" Jason asked the captain of this guard, a surly brute named Benn't.

"Unnh," Benn't answered, and led the way into the drafty Perssonoj keep. They went up a tortuous stone staircase that led to the higher floors, then down a dark hall to a solid door where another guard was stationed. Benn't opened it with a heavy key that hung from his belt.

"This yours," he spat, with a jerk of his black-nailed thumb.

"Complete with slaves," Jason said, looking in and seeing Mikah and Ijale chained to the wall. "I'm not going to get much work out of those two if they are just being used as decorations. Do you have the key?"

With even less grace, Benn't dug a smaller key from his wallet and passed it to Jason; then he went out and locked the door behind him.

"I knew you would do something so they would not hurt you," Ijale said as Jason unlocked her iron collar. "I only feared a little bit."

Mikah maintained a stony silence until Jason began an inspection round of the rooms with Ijale, then he said coldly, "You have neglected to free me from these chains."

"I'm glad you noticed that," Jason said. "It saves my bringing it to your attention. Can you think of a better way to keep you out of trouble?"

"You are insulting!"

"I'm truthful. You lost me my steady job with the *d'zertanoj* and had me locked up as a slave. When I escaped I took you with me, and you repaid my generosity by allowing Snarbi to betray us to my present employer—and this position I obtained with no thanks to you."

"I did only what I thought was best."

"You thought wrong."

"You are a vindictive and petty man, Jason dinAlt!"

"You're damned right. You stay chained to that wall."

Jason put his arm through Ijale's and took her on a guided tour of the apartment. "In the most modern fashion the entrance opens directly into the main chamber, furnished with rustic split-log furniture and walls decorated with a fine variety of molds. A great place to make cheese, but unfit for human habitation. We'll let Mikah have it." He opened a connecting door. "This is more like it, a southern exposure, a view of the grand canal, and a bit of light. Windows of the best cracked horn, admitting both sunshine and fresh air. I'll have to put some glass in here. But right now a fire in that ox-roasting fireplace will have to do."

"*Krenoj!*" Ijale squealed, and ran to a basket set in an alcove. Jason shuddered. She smelled a few, pinching them between her fingers. "Not too old, ten days, maybe fifteen. Good for soup."

"Just what the old stomach yearns for," Jason said unenthusiastically.

Mikah bellowed from the other room. Jason started the fire before he went to see what he wanted.

"This is criminal!" Mikah said, rattling his chains.

"I'm a criminal." Jason turned to leave.

"Wait! You cannot leave me like this. We are civilized men. Release me and I will give you my word that I bear you no ill will."

"That's very nice of you, Mikah old son, but all the trust is gone from my previously trusting soul. I am a convert to the native ethos, and I now trust you as far as I can see you. I'll give you that much. You can have the run of the place just to stop your bellowing."

Jason unlocked the chain that secured Mikah's iron collar to the wall, then turned away.

"You have forgotten the collar," Mikah said.

"Have I?" Jason answered, and his grin was more predatory than humorous. "I haven't forgotten how you betrayed me to Edipon, nor have I forgotten the collar. As long as you are a slave you cannot betray me again—so a slave you stay."

"I should have expected this of you." There was cold fury in Mikah's voice. "You are a dog, not a civilized man. I will *not* give you my word to assist you in any way; I am ashamed of myself for my weakness in even considering such a course. You are evil, and my life is dedicated to fighting evil—therefore I fight you."

Jason had his arm half-raised to strike, but instead he burst out laughing.

"You never cease to amaze me, Mikah. It seems impossible that one man could be so insensitive to facts, logic, reality, or what used to be called plain common sense. I'm glad you admitted that you are fighting me—it will make it easier to guard my back. And just so you won't forget and start acting chummy again, I'm keeping you a slave and treating you like a slave. So grab that stoneware crock over there and

117

hammer for the guard and go fill it with water wherever slaves like you go to fetch water."

He turned on his heels and left the room, still seething with anger, but he tried to work up some enthusiasm for the meal Ijale had so carefully prepared.

With a full stomach and his feet toasting by the fire, Jason was almost comfortable. Ijale was crouched by the hearth doing a slow and clumsy job of repairing some skins with a large iron needle, while from the other room came the angry rattle of Mikah's chains. It was late and Jason was tired, but he had promised the Hertug a list of possible wonders and he wanted to finish it before he went to sleep. He looked up as the locks on the front entrance rattled open and the guard officer Benn't stamped in, followed by one of his soldiers, who carried a spluttering torch.

"Come," Benn't said, and pointed to the door.

"Where and why?" Jason asked, reluctant to face the damp discomfort of the keep.

"Come," Benn't repeated in the same unpleasant tone, and pulled his short stabbing sword from his belt.

"I'm learning to loathe you," Jason said, dragging himself reluctantly to his feet. He slipped his fur vest back on and went out past Mikah's brooding form. The guard at the door was gone and there was a dark shape on the floor just visible in the torchlight. Was it the guard? Jason started to turn when the door slammed behind them and the point of Benn't's sword jammed through his leather clothes and pinked the skin over his kidneys.

"Talk or move, you die," the soldier's voice grated in his ear.

Jason thought about it and decided not to move. Not that the threat disturbed him, for he was sure he could disarm Benn't and reach the other soldier before he could draw his sword, but he was interested in this new development. He had more than a strong suspicion that what was happening was unknown to the Hertug, and he wondered just where it would lead.

He regretted his decision instantly. A foul-tasting rag was stuffed into his mouth and tied in place with straps that cut into his neck and jaws. His arms were tied at the same moment and a second sword was pressed into his side. Resistance was impossible now, without serious risk, so he marched humbly up the stairs when prodded, and out onto the flat roof of the building.

The soldier put out his torch and they were in the black night, cold sleet blowing about them. They stumbled across the slippery tiles. The parapet was invisible in the darkness and when it hit Jason's legs just below the knees he tottered and would have gone over if the soldiers hadn't dragged him back. Working silently and swiftly, they knotted a rope under his arms and lowered him over the edge. Jason cursed inside the gag as he bumped painfully down the rough outer facing of the building, then recoiled as he went up to his knees in icy water. This side of the Perssonoj keep dropped sheer to the canal and Jason hung there, immersed to his waist, as the barely visible shape of a boat loomed out of the sleet-filled darkness. Rough hands pulled him in and dumped him down, and a few moments later the boat rocked as his kidnappers descended the rope and dropped in beside him. Oars squeaked and they moved off. No alarm had been raised.

The men in the boat ignored him; in fact, they used him for a footrest until he squirmed away. There was little enough to see, lying flat as he was, until more flares appeared and he saw that they were rowing through a large sea gate, much like the one at the entrance to the Perssonoj keep. It did not take much deliberation to realize that he had been picked up by one of the competing organizations. When the boat stopped he was thrown onto the dock, then hauled through damp stone halls to face a high, rusty iron portal. Benn't had vanished—probably after receiving his thirty pieces of silver—and the new guards were silent. They untied him, pulled the gag from his mouth, pushed him through the iron door, and slammed it shut behind him. He was left alone to face the spine-chilling terrors of the chamber.

There were seven figures seated on a high dais, robed, armoured, and fearfully masked. Each leaned on a meter-long broadsword. Oddly shaped lamps burned and smoked about them and the air was thick with the reek of hydrogen sulphide.

Jason laughed coldly and looked around for a chair. None was visible, so he took a sputtering lamp, shaped like a snake with a flame in its mouth, from a nearby table and put it on the floor, and then sat on the table. He turned a contemptuous eye on the horrors before him.

"Stand, mortal!" the central figure said. "To sit before the Mastreguloj is death!"

"I sit," Jason said, making himself comfortable. "You didn't kidnap me just to kill me, and the sooner you realize that horror-comic outfits don't bother me, the quicker we will be able to get down to business."

"Silence! Death is at hand!"

"*Ekskremento*!" Jason sneered. "Your masks and threats are of about the same quality as those of the desert slavers. Let's get down to facts. You have been collecting rumors about me and they have got you interested. You have heard about the supercharged *caro*, and spies have told you about the electronic prayer wheel in the temple—maybe more. It all sounded so good that you wanted me for yourselves, and you tried the foolproof Appsalan dodge of a little money in the right places. And here I am."

"Do you know to whom you talk?" the masked figure on the far right asked in a high-pitched, shaking voice. Jason examined the speaker carefully.

"The Mastreguloj? I've heard about you. You are supposed to be the witches and warlocks of this town, with fire that burns in water, smoke that will burn the lungs, water that will burn the flesh, and so forth. My guess is that you are the local equivalents of chemists; and though there aren't supposed to be very many of you, you are nasty enough to keep the other tribes frightened."

"Do you know what this contains?" the man asked, holding up a glass sphere with some yellowish liquid in it.

"I don't know, and I couldn't care less."

"It contains the magic burning water that will sear you and char you in an instant if it touches—"

"Oh, come off it! There's nothing in there but some common acid, probably sulphuric, because the other acids are made from it, and there is also the strong clue of rotten egg reek that fills this room."

His guess seemed to have struck home; the seven figures stirred and muttered to each other. While they were distracted, Jason stood up and walked slowly towards them. He had had enough of the scientific quiz game and felt bitter about being kidnapped, tied, dunked, and walked on. These Mastreguloj were feared and avoided by the others in

Appsala, but they weren't a large enough clan for what he had in mind. For a number of good reasons he had backed the Perssonoj to win and he wasn't changing sides now.

Among the trivia cluttering the back of his mind was a statement he had read once in a book about famous escapes. He had noted it because he had a professional interest in escaping, since, on many occasions his aims and the police's had differed. The conclusion he had reached by a study of escapees was that the best time to escape was as soon as possible after you have been captured. Which was now.

The Mastreguloj had made a mistake by seeing him alone; they were so used to cowing and frightening people that they were getting careless—and old. From their voices and from the way they acted, he was sure that there were no young men on the dais, and he was equally certain that the man on the right end was well into senility. His voice had revealed it, and now that Jason was closer he could see the palsied vibration that shook the large sword the man held before him.

"Who revealed the secret and sacred name of *sulfurika acido*?" the central figure boomed. "Speak, spy, or we will have your tongue torn from your head, fire poured into your bowels—"

"Don't do that," Jason pleaded, kneeling and clasping his hands prayerfully before him. "Anything but that! I'll talk!" He shuffled forward on his knees closer to the dais, bearing to the right as he did so. "The truth will out, I can no longer conceal it—here is the man who told me all the sacred secrets." He pointed to the oldster on the right, and when he did so his hand came close to the long sword the man held.

As Jason stood up, he reached out and plucked the sword from the old man's loose grip and pushed him sideways into the next chair—both men went over with a satisfactory crash.

"Death to unbelievers!" he shouted, and pulled down the black hanging with skull-and-demon pattern that covered the back wall. He threw it over the two men near him, who were just struggling to their feet, and he saw a small door that had been concealed behind the drapery. Pushing it open, he jumped through into the lamplit corridor beyond and almost into the arms of the two guards stationed there.

The benefit of surprise was on his side. The first one collapsed when Jason rapped him on the head with the flat of his blade, and the second dropped his own sword when Jason's point took him in the upper arm. His Pyrran training was serving him now. He could move faster and kill quicker than any of the Appsalans. He proved this when he ran around a corner, going in the direction of the entrance, and almost ran into Benn't, his former guard.

"Thanks for bringing me here—I didn't have enough troubles," Jason said, beating the other's sword aside. "And while being a paid traitor is normal in Appsala, it wasn't nice to kill one of your own men." His sword swung and tore Benn't's throat open, almost taking his head off at the same time. The broadsword was heavy and hard to swing, but once it started moving it sliced through anything in its way. Jason ran on and enthusiastically attacked the guards in the front hall.

The only advantage he had was again the element of surprise, so he moved as fast as he could. Once they united, they could capture and kill him, but it was late at night and the last thing the bored guards expected was this demoniacal attack from their rear. One went down, another staggered away with blood spouting from a butchered arm, and Jason was throwing his weight on the pivoted bar that sealed the entrance. From the corner of his eye he saw one of the masked Mastreguloj appear from the council room by way of the main entrance.

"Die!" the man shrieked, and hurled a glass sphere at Jason's head.

"Thanks," Jason said, catching the thing neatly in midair with his free hand. He slipped it inside his clothes as he pulled the door open.

Pursuit was just being organized when he ran down the slippery stairs and jumped into the nearest boat. It was too large for him to row easily, but he cut the painter and pushed off with a leaf-shaped oar. There was a sluggish tide moving in the channel, and he let it carry him away as he dropped the oars on the tholepins and pulled lustily. Figures appeared on the stairs, there were shouts and the flicker of torches, then a cloud of sleet blew in between and they were lost from view. Jason rowed on into the darkness, smiling to himself.

CHAPTER THIRTEEN

He rowed until the exercise warmed him, then let the boat drift with the tide. It bumped against unseen obstacles in the dark, and whirled about when it came to another canal. Jason pulled lustily into this, and made his way through a maze of dimly seen waterways between low islands and cliff-like walls. When he was sure his trail was sufficiently confused he pulled to the nearest shore where he could beach the boat. It came to a stop and he jumped out, ankle deep in the wet sand, and he pulled it as far up as he could.

When he could no longer move it he climbed back in, put the glass capsule out of reach in the bilge where it could not be broken accidentally, and settled down to wait for dawn. He was chilled and shivering, and before the first grey light penetrated the sleet he was in a foul humor.

Dim shapes slowly resolved themselves from the darkness —some small boats nearby, drawn up on shore and securely chained to piles, and further back small, squat buildings. A man crawled from one of the hovels, but as soon as he saw Jason and his boat he squealed and vanished from sight. There were stirrings and mumblings inside, and Jason climbed out onto the shore and swung the broadsword a few times to loosen up his muscles.

About a dozen men came hesitantly down to the shore to face him, clutching clubs and oars, almost shivering with fright.

"Go, leave us in peace," the leader said, extending his index finger and little finger to avert the evil eye. "Take your foul bark, Mastregulo, and depart our shore. We are but poor fisherfolk . . ."

"I have nothing but sympathy for you," Jason said, leaning on the sword. "And I have no more love for the Mastreguloj than you have."

"But your boat—there is the sign," and the leader pointed to a hideous bit of carving on the bow.

"I stole it from them."

The fishermen moaned and milled about, some running away, while a few dropped to their knees to pray. One threw his club at Jason, a half-hearted attempt that Jason parried easily with his sword.

"We are lost," the leader wailed. "The Mastreguloj will follow, sight this craft of ill omen, and fall upon us and kill us all. Take it, leave at once!"

"There's something in what you say," Jason agreed. The boat was a handicap. He could barely manage it alone and it was too easily identified to enable him to move about unnoticed. Keeping a wary eye on the fishermen, he retrieved the glass ball and then put his shoulder to the bow, sliding the boat back into the water, where the current caught it and soon carried it out of sight.

"That problem is taken care of," Jason said. "Now I have to get back to the Perssonoj stronghold. Which of you wants the ferry job?"

The fishermen began to drift away, and Jason planted himself in front of the leader before he could vanish too. "Well, how about it?"

"I don't think I could find it," the man said, going white under his wind-burned skin. "Fog, plenty of sleet, I never go that way ..."

"Come on, now, you'll be well paid, just as soon as we land. Name your price."

The man gave a mean laugh and tried to edge away.

"I see what you mean," Jason said, putting his sword in the other's way. "Credit is one custom that doesn't mean much here."

Jason looked thoughtfully at the sword and realized for the first time that the bumps on the hilt were faceted stones in ornate settings. He pointed to them. "Here we go, payment in advance if you can find me a knife to pry these out with. As a down payment, that red one that looks like a ruby; then the green one when we get there."

With a bit of arguing, and the addition of another red stone avarice won over fear, as usual, and the fisherman pushed a small and badly joined boat into the canal. He rowed while Jason bailed and they began a surreptitious tour of the back canals. Aided by sleet, fog, and the fisherman's suddenly regained and intimate knowledge of the waterways, they arrived unobserved at some crumbled stone steps leading to a barred gate. The man swore that this was an entrance to the Perssonoj stronghold. Jason, well versed in local custom by now, was aware that it might be something quite different, even a way to the Mastreguloj he had just left, and he kept one foot in the boat until a guard appeared with the characteristic Perssonoj sunburst on his cloak. The fisherman received the final payment with astonishment and rowed quickly away, muttering to himself. Another guard was called, Jason's sword was taken from him, and he was quickly brought to the Hertug's audience chamber.

"Traitor!" the Hertug shouted, dispensing with all formalities. "You conspire to kill my men and flee, but I have you now—"

"Oh, stop it!" Jason said irritably, and shrugged away the guards who were holding his arms. "I returned voluntarily, and that should mean something, even in Appsala. I was kidnapped by the Mastreguloj, with the aid of a traitor in your guard—"

"His name!"

"Benn't, deceased—I saw to that myself. Your trusted captain sold you out to the competition, who wanted me to work for them, but I didn't accept. I didn't think too much of their outfit and I left before they got around to making an offer. But I brought a sample back with me." Jason pulled out the glass sphere of acid and the guards dropped back, screaming, and even Hertug went white.

"The burning water!" he gasped.

"Exactly. And as soon as I get some lead it is going to become part of the wet cell battery I was busy inventing. I'm annoyed, Hertug—I don't like being kidnaped and pushed around. Everything about Appsala annoys me, and I have some plans for the future. Clear these men out so I can tell my plans to you."

The Hertug chewed his lip nervously and looked at the guards. "You came back," he said to Jason—"why?"

"Because I need you just as much as you need me. You have plenty of men, power, and money. I have big plans. Now clear the serfs out."

There was a bowl of *krenoj* on the table and Jason rooted around for a fresh one and bit off a piece. The Hertug was thinking hard.

"You came back," he said again. He seemed to find this fact astonishing. "Let us talk."

"Alone."

"Clear the chamber," he ordered, but he took the precaution of having a cocked crossbow placed before him. Jason ignored it; he had expected no less. He crossed to the badly glazed window and looked out at the island city. The storm had stopped finally, and weak sunshine was lighting up the rain-darkened roofs.

"How would you like to own all that?" Jason asked.

"Speak on." The Hertug's little eyes glittered.

"I mentioned this before, but now I mean it—seriously. I am going to reveal to you every secret of every other clan on this damned planet. I'm going to show you how the *d'zertanoj* distill oil, how the Mastreguloj make sulphuric acid, how the Trozelligoj build engines. Then I'm going to improve your weapons of war, and introduce as many new ones as I can. I will make war so terrible that it will no longer be possible. Of course it will still go on, but your troops will always win. You'll wipe out the competition, one by one, starting with the weakest ones, until you will be the master of this city, then of the whole planet. The riches of a world will be yours, and your evenings will be enlivened by the horrible deaths you will mete out to your enemies. What do you say?"

"*Supren la Perssonoj!*" the Hertug shouted, leaping to his feet.

"That's what I thought you would say. If I'm going to be stuck here for any length of time I want to get in a few body blows to the system. I have been entirely too uncomfortable, and it is time for a change."

CHAPTER FOURTEEN

The days grew longer, the sleet turned to rain, but even that finally stopped. The last clouds eventually blew out to sea and the sun shone down on the city of Appsala. Buds opened, flowers blossomed and filled the air with perfume, while from the warming waters of the canals there rose another odor, less pleasant, that Jason could just as well have done without. But he had very little time to notice it, for he was working long hours at both research and production, a constantly exhausting task. Pure research and production development were expensive, and when the bills mounted too high the Hertug scratched in his beard and mumbled about the good old days. Then Jason had to drop everything and produce a fresh miracle or two. The arc light was one; then the arc furnace, which helped with the metallurgical work and made the Hertug very happy, particularly when he found out how good it was for torture and fed a captured Trozelligo into it until he told them what they wanted to know. When this novelty palled, Jason introduced electroplating, which helped fill the treasury both through jewelry sales and counterfeiting.

After opening the Mastreguloj glass sphere with elaborate precautions, Jason satisfied himself that it did contain sulphuric acid, and he constructed a heavy, but effective storage battery. Still angry over the kidnaping, he led an attack on a Mastreguloj barge and captured a large supply of acid, as well as assorted other chemicals. These he was testing whenever he had the time. He had followed a number of dead-end trials, but had been forced to abandon them. The formula for gunpowder escaped him, and this depressed him, though it cheered his assistants who had been raking through old manure piles for supplies of saltpeter.

He had more success with *caroj* and steam engines, because of previous experience, and developed a lightweight sturdy marine engine. In his spare moments he invented movable type, the telephone, and the loudspeaker—which, with the addition of the phonograph record, did wonders for the religious revenues in production of spirit voices. He also made a naval propeller to go with his engine, and was busily perfecting a steam catapult. For his own pleasure he had set up a still in his rooms, with which he manufactured a coarse but effective brandy.

"All in all, things aren't going too badly," he said, lolling back in his upholstered easy chair and sipping a glass of his latest and best. It had been a warm day, and more than a bit choking with the effluvia that rose from the canals, but now the evening sea breeze was cool and sweet as it blew in through the open windows. Under his belt was a fine steak cooked on a charcoal grill of his own invention, served with mashed *krenoj* and bread baked from flour ground in his recently invented mill. Ijale was singing in the kitchen as she cleaned up, and Mikah was industriously running a brush through the pipes of the still, clearing away the dregs of the last batch.

"Sure you won't join me in a quick one?" Jason asked, brimming with the milk of human kindness.

"Wine is a mocker, strong drink is raging . . . Proverbs," Mikah declaimed in his best style.

"Wine that maketh glad the heart of man. Psalms. I've read the Book too. But if you won't have a friendly cup, why don't you have a refreshing glass of water and take a rest? That job can wait until morning."

"I am your slave," Mikah said darkly, touching the iron collar about his neck for an instant, then turning back to his work.

"Well, you have only yourself to blame. If you were more trustworthy I would give you your freedom. In fact, why don't I do that? Just give me your word that you'll not cook up any more trouble, and I'll have you out of that collar before you can say antidisestablishmentarianism. I think I'm in well enough with the Hertug to ride any minor troubles you might cause. What do you say? As narrow-minded as your conversation is, it's at least twice as good as anything else I can find on this planet."

Mikah touched the collar again and looked doubtful for just a moment. Then he shouted "No!" and jerked his fingers away as if they were burnt. "Behind me, Satan! Down! I will give you no pledges, nor will I put my honor in fief to such as you. Better to serve in bondage until the day of liberation when I will see you standing trial for such crimes as this, standing before a bar of justice, being sentenced and doomed."

"Well, you leave little doubt as to your ambitions." Jason drained the glass appreciatively and refilled it. "I hope they work out, at least the day of liberation part; after that I find our opinions of the correct course differ a little. But have you ever stopped to think how far away that day of liberation may be? And just what are you doing to bring it about?"

"I can do nothing—I am a slave!"

"Yes, and we both know why. But aside from that, do you think you could do any better if you were free? I'll answer for you. No. But I can do better, and I have come up with a few answers. For one thing, there are no offworlders besides us on this forsaken planet. I found some crystals that resonate nicely and I built a crystal radio. I didn't hear a thing except atmospherics and my own holy S.O.S."

"What blasphemy do you speak?"

"Didn't I ever tell you? I built a simple radio disguised as an electronic prayer wheel and the faithful have been broadcasting religiously since the first day."

"Is nothing sacred to you, blasphemer?"

"We'll go into that some other time—though I can't see what you are complaining about now. Do you mean you *respect* this phoney religion with great god Elektro and all the rest? You should be thankful that I am getting some productive mileage out of the worshipers. If any spacer ever gets near the atmosphere of this planet, it will pick up the call for help and head this way."

"How soon?" Mikah asked, interested in spite of himself.

"It could be in five minutes—or in five hundred years. Even if someone is looking for you, there are a lot of planets in this galaxy. I doubt if the Pyrrans will come after me—they have only one spaceship and have plenty of uses for it. What about your people?"

"They will pray for me, but they cannot search. Most of our money was used to obtain the ship you so willfully destroyed. But what of other ships? Surely traders, explorers . . ."

"Chance—it depends completely on the hazards of chance. As I said, five minutes from now, five centuries—or never. The blind workings of chance."

Mikah sat down heavily, wrapped in gloom, and Jason—despite the fact that he realized he should know better—felt a momentary pang of pity. "But cheer up, things aren't that bad here," he said. "Just compare our present position with our first job *kreno* hunting in Ch'aka's merry band. Now we have a place with comfortable furnishings, heating, good food, and, as fast as I can invent them, all the modern conveniences. For my own comfort, plus the fact that I hate so many of the people involved, I am going to drag this world out of its dark age and get it headed into the glories of the technological future. Did you think I was going to all this trouble just to help the Hertug?"

"I do not understand."

"That's fairly typical. Look, we have here a static culture that is never going to change without a large charge of explosive put in the proper place. That's me. As long as knowledge is classified as an official secret, there will be no advance. There will probably be slight modifications and improvements within these clans as they work on their specialities, but nothing of any vital importance. I'm ruining all that. I'm letting our Hertug have the information possessed by every other tribe, plus a lot of gadgets they don't know about yet. This destroys the normal check and balance that keeps these warring mobs roughly equal, and if he runs his war right—meaning my way—he can pick them off one by one . . ."

"War?" Mikah asked, his nostrils flaring, the old light back in his eyes. "Did you say *war*?"

"That's the word," Jason answered, complacently sipping at his glass, drunk with his own vision and half-stoned on the home brew, so that he did not notice the warning signs. "As someone once said, you can't make an omelet without breaking eggs. Left alone, this world will stumble on its orbit forever with ninety-nine per cent of the population doomed to disease, poverty, filth, misery, slavery, and all the rest. I'm going to start a war, a nice, clean scientific one that will wipe out the competition. When it is all over this will be a far, far better place for everyone. The Hertug will have cleaned up the other mobs and will be dictator. The work I am doing is already too much for the ancient *sciuloj*, and I have been subcontracting to slaves and training younger technicians from the family. When I am through there will be a cross-fertilization of all the sciences, and industrial revolution will be in full swing here. There will be no turning back, because the old ways will be dead. Machines, capital, entrepreneurs, leisure, the arts . . ."

"You are a monster!" Mikah rasped through his teeth. "To satisfy your own ego you would even start war and condemn thousands of innocents to death. I will stop you, if it costs me my life!"

"Whazzat . . .?" Jason said, lifting his head. He had drifted off to sleep, worn out from work and lulled by his own golden vision.

But Mikah did not answer. He had his back turned and was bent over the still, cleaning it. His face was flushed and his teeth were clamped so hard into his lip that a thin trickle of blood ran down his chin. He had finally learned the benefits of silence at certain times, though the effort of maintaining it was almost killing him.

In the courtyard of the Perssonoj keep was a great stone tank kept filled with fresh water pumped from barges. Here the slaves met as they drew their supplies, and here was the center of gossip—and intrigue. Mikah waited his turn at the tap to fill his bucket, but at the same time he examined the faces of the other slaves, looking for the one who had talked to him a few weeks earlier, whom he had ignored at the time. He finally saw him, dragging in faggots of firewood from the unloading dock, and went over to him.

"I will help," Mikah whispered as he passed. The man smiled crookedly.

"At last you are being wise. All will be arranged."

It was full summer. The days were hot and humid, the air cooling off only after dark. Jason had reached the proving stages of his steam catapult when he was forced to violate his rule of doing only day work. At the last minute he decided on an evening test, since with the oil-fired boiler working full blast the heat was unbearable during the daytime. Mikah had gone out for water to refill their kitchen tank—he had forgotten it during the day—so Jason did not see him when he went down to the workshop after dinner. Jason's assistants had the boiler hot and a head of steam up: the tests began. Because of the hiss of leaking steam and the general uproar of the mechanism, the first sign he had that anything was wrong was when a soldier burst in with blood soaking his leather from a crossbow quarrel stuck in his shoulder.

"Attacking—Trozelligoj!" he gasped.

Jason shouted orders, but was ignored in the concerted rush to the door. Cursing, he stayed long enough to damp the fire and open a bleed valve so the boiler wouldn't blow up while he was away. Then he followed the others out of the door, going by way of the rack that held his experimental weapons, and without stopping he pulled from it a newly constructed morning star, an ugly-looking weapon consisting of a thick handle surmounted by a bronze ball into which were set machined steel spikes. It balanced nicely in the hand and whistled in the air when he swung it.

He ran through the dark halls toward the sounds of distant shouting, which seemed to be coming from the courtyard. As he went by the stairs that led to the upper floors, he was vaguely aware of a clatter from somewhere above, and a muffled shout. Going out the wide main entrance that opened onto the courtyard, he saw that the battle was in its final stages and would be won without any help from him.

Carbon arcs lit the scene with a harsh light. The sea gate leading into the pool had been crashed partly open by a barge with a pointed prow, which still remained there, caught fast in the splintered gates. Unable to force their way into the courtyard, the Trozelligoj had attacked along the wall and wiped out most of the guard there. But before they could reach the courtyard and bring reinforcements over the wall, the counterattack of the aroused defenders had halted them. Success was now impossible and they were retreating slowly, fighting a rear-guard action. Men were still dying, but the battle was over. Corpses, most of them studded with bolts from the crossbows, floated in the water, and the wounded were already being dragged away. There was nothing much here that Jason could do, and he wondered what reason lay behind the midnight attack.

At the same moment he felt a presentiment of further trouble clutch at his insides. What was wrong? The attack was beaten off, yet he felt that something was not right, something important. Then he remembered the sounds he had heard coming down the stairwell—heavy feet and the clattering of weapons. And the shout, cut off as if someone had been silenced. The sounds had meant little when he heard them; if he had thought about them at all he had assumed that more soldiers were coming to join in the battle.

"But I was the last one to come through this door! No

one came down the stairs!" Even as he was saying the words, he was running towards the stairs, and he bounded up them three at a time.

There was a crash from somewhere above, and the clank of metal on stone. Jason burst out into the hallway, stumbling and half falling over a body huddled there, and he realized that the sounds of fighting were coming from his own rooms.

Inside them it was a madhouse, a slaughterhouse; only one lamp lay unbroken, and in its uncertain light soldiers stumbled over the crushed remains of his furnishings, struggled, and died. The rooms seemed smaller, filled now with fighting men, and Jason leaped over a pair of tangled corpses to join the thin ranks of the Perssonoj.

"Ijale," he shouted, "where are you?" and swung the morning star against the helmet of a charging soldier. The man went down, taking another with him, and Jason jumped into the opening.

"There is the one!" a voice shouted from the rear ranks of the Trozelligoj, and Jason was almost swamped as the attackers turned their attention to him. There were so many of them that they got in each other's way as they pressed the attack home with desperate fury. They were trying to disable him, attempting to cut his legs from under him or put a crossbow bolt through his arm. A sword sliced into his calf before he could deflect it, and his arm ached with the effort needed to keep the morning star a twirling web of death in front of him. He was aware of the desperate men who were attacking him, and did not know that word of this raid had spread and that more defenders had arrived until the soldiers in front of him were swept back by a rush of Perssonoj.

Jason wiped the sweat from his eyes with his sleeve and stumbled after them. There were more torches now, and he could see that the outnumbered raiders were in retreat, fighting a rear-guard defense shoulder to shoulder while others struggled to get through the wide windows that faced the canal. His carefully installed glass panes were now broken shards underfoot, while hooks and grappling irons were sunk into the frame and wall, and thick ropes passed out through the opening.

A crossbow squad rushed in and brought down the last of the rear-guard and Jason led the rush to the window.

Dark forms were vanishing out of sight down the wall, clambering in desperate haste down the hanging rope ladders. The shouting victors began to saw through the ropes until Jason knocked them aside with a sweep of his arm.

"No—follow them!" he shouted, and swung his leg over the windowsill. With the haft of the morning star clutched in his teeth, he climbed down the swaying rope ladder, cursing indistinctly its swaying rungs.

When he reached the bottom he saw that the ends of the ropes trailed in the water, and he could hear the sound of hurried oars vanishing in the darkness.

Jason was suddenly and painfully aware of his wounded leg, as well as of his state of exhaustion : he was not going to attempt to climb back up.

"Have them bring a boat around," he told the soldier who had followed him down. Then he hung there, his arm hooked over a rung, until the boat appeared. The Hertug himself was in the bow, a naked sword in his hand.

"What is this attack? What is the meaning of it?" the Hertug demanded. Jason hauled himself wearily into the boat and sank onto a bench.

"It's obvious enough now—the whole attack was just meant to get me."

"What? It cannot be . . ."

"It certainly is, if you just look at it closely for a moment. The attack on the sea gate was never meant to succeed; it was just a distraction while the real plan to kidnap me was pushed through. It was only chance that I was working in the shop tonight—I'm usually asleep by this time."

"Who would want you? Why?"

"Haven't you waked up to the fact yet that I'm the most valuable piece of property in Appsala? The Mastreguloj were the first to realize that; they even successfully kidnaped me, as you may remember. We should have been alert for a Trozelligoj attack; after all, they must know by now that I'm making steam engines, their old monopoly."

The boat swung in through the splintered sea gate and ground against the dock, and Jason swung painfully ashore.

"But how did they get in and find your quarters?" the Hertug asked.

"It was an inside job, a traitor, as always on this pest-ridden planet. Someone who knew the routine, who could set the hook and drop the first ladder down to the waiting boats just before the attack. It wasn't Ijale—they must have captured her."

"I will discover who the traitor is!" the Hertug raged. "I'll feed him into the arc furnace an inch at a time."

"I know who it is," Jason told him, and there was an ugly glitter in his eye. "I heard his voice when I came in, telling them who I was. I recognized the voice—it was my slave, Mikah."

CHAPTER FIFTEEN

"They'll pay—oh, how they'll pay for this!" the Hertug growled, grating his teeth together with a horrible sound. He was sipping at a glass of Jason's brandy, and his eyes and nose were even redder than usual.

"I'm glad to hear you say that, because it's just what I had in mind," Jason said, leaning back on a couch with an even bigger glass balanced on his chest. He had washed out the cut on his leg with boiled water and bound it with sterile bandages. It was throbbing a bit now, but he doubted if it would give him much trouble. He ignored it and made his plans. "Let's start the war now," he said.

The Hertug blinked. "Isn't that sudden? I mean, are we ready yet?"

"They invaded your castle, killed your soldiers, wrecked your—"

"Death to the Trozelligoj!" the Hertug screamed and crashed his glass against the wall.

"That's more like it. Don't forget what stab-in-the-back bastards they are, pulling a stunt like this. You can't let them get away with it. Plus the fact that we had better start the war soon, or we will never have a chance. If the Trozelligoj will go to this much trouble to grab me, they must be very worried. Since this plan didn't succeed, they will be thinking next of a stronger attack—and will probably get some of the other clans to help with it. They are all beginning to fear you, Hertug, so we had better get the war rolling before they decide to get together and wipe us out. We can still take the clans on, one at a time, and be sure of victory."

"It would help if we had more men, and a little time . . ."

"We have about two days—that's as long as it will take me to equip my invasion fleet. That will give you enough time to call in the reserves from the country. Strip the estates, because we want to attack and take the Trozelligoj fortress, and this is the only chance we will have. And the new steam catapult will do the job."

"It has been tested?"

"Just enough to show it will do what it was designed to do.

We can do the ranging and sighting with the Trozelligoj for a target. I'll start work at first light, but I suggest that you get the messengers out now so that the men can get here in plenty of time. Death to the Trozelligoj!"

"Death!" the Hertug echoed, and he grimaced horribly as he rang for the servant.

There was much to be done, and Jason accomplished it by going without sleep. When he became tired he would think about the treacherous Mikah, and wonder what had happened to Ijale, and anger would drive him back to work. He had no assurance that Ijale was even alive; he just assumed that she had been kidnaped as part of his household. As for Mikah, he was going to have a lot to answer for.

Because the steam engine and propeller had already been installed in a ship and tested inside the sea gates, finishing the warship did not take very long. It was mostly a matter of bolting on the iron plates he had designed to shield it down to the waterline. The plating was thicker at the bow, and he saw to it that heavier internal bracing was installed. At first he had thought to install the steam catapult on the warship, but then had decided against it. A simpler way was better. The catapult was fitted into a large, flat-bottomed barge, along with the boiler, tanks of fuel, and a selection of carefully designed missiles.

The Perssonoj were pouring in, all of them fuming with anger over the back-stabbing attack and thirsting for vengeance. In spite of their shouting Jason snatched a few hours' sleep on the second night and had himself waked at dawn. The fleet was assembled, and with much drum-beating and off-key bugling they set sail.

First came the warship, the "Dreadnaught", with Jason and the Hertug on its armored bridge; this towed the barge. In line astern were a great variety of vessels of all sizes, loaded with troops. The entire city knew what was happening and the canals were deserted, while the Trozelligoj fortress was sealed, barred, and waiting. Jason let go a blast of the steam whistle, well out of arrow range of the enemy walls, and the fleet reluctantly halted.

"Why don't we attack?" the Hertug asked.

"Because we have them in range, while they can't reach us. See." Immense, iron-headed spears plunged into the water a good thirty meters from the bow of the ship.

"*Jetilo* arrows." The Hertug shuddered. "I've seen them

pass through the bodies of seven men without being slowed."

"Not this time. I'm about to show you the glories of scientific warfare."

The fire from the *jetiloj* was no more effective than the shouting soldiers on the walls who were clashing swords on shields and hurling curses, and it soon stopped. Jason transferred to the barge and saw that it was anchored firmly, pointing its bow directly at the fortress. While the steam pressure was building up, he aimed the centerline of the catapult and took a guess at the elevation.

The device was simple, but powerful, and he had high hopes for it. On the platform, which could be rotated and elevated, was mounted a single large steam cylinder with its piston connected directly to the short arm of a long lever. When steam was admitted to the cylinder, the short but immensely powerful stroke of the piston was turned by mechanical advantage into flailing speed at the far end of the arm. This whipped up and crashed into a padded crossarm and was stopped, but whatever load was placed in the cup on the end of the arm went speeding off through the air. The mechanism had been tested and worked perfectly, though no shots had yet been fired.

"Full pressure," Jason called out to his technicians. "Load one of the stones into the cup." He had prepared a variety of missiles, all of them weighing the same in order to simplify ranging problems. While the weapon was being loaded he checked the flexible steam lines once more : they had been the hardest thing to manufacture, and they still had a tendency to leak under pressure and continued use.

"Here goes !" he shouted, and pulled down on the valve.

The piston drove out with a satisfactory speed, the arm whipped up and crashed resoundingly into the stop—while the stone went whistling away, a dwindling dot. All the Perssonoj cheered. But the cheering stopped when the stone kept on going, clearing the topmost turret of the keep by a good fifty meters, and vanished on the other side. The Trozelligoj burst into raucous cheering of their own when it splashed harmlessly into the canal on the far side.

"Just a ranging shot," Jason said offhandedly. "A little less elevation and I'll drop one like a bomb into their courtyard."

He cracked the exhaust valves and gravity drew the long arm back to the horizontal, at the same time returning the

138

piston for the next shot. Jason carefully shut the valve and cranked on the elevation wheel. A stone was loaded and he fired again.

This time only the Trozelligoj fortress cheered as the stone mounted almost straight up, then dropped to sink one of the attacking boats less than fifty meters from the barge.

"I do not think much of your devilish machine," the Hertug said. He had come back to watch the firing.

"There are always field problems," Jason answered through tight lips. "Just watch the next shot." He decided to abandon any more attempts at fancy high trajectories, and to let fly head-on, for the machine was far more powerful than he had estimated. Cranking furiously on the elevation wheel, he raised the rear of the catapult until the stone would leave the cup almost parallel with the water.

"This is the shot that tells," he announced with much more conviction than he felt, and crossed the fingers of his free hand as he fired. The stone hummed away and hit just below the top of the crenellated wall. It blasted out a great chunk of masonry and utterly demolished the soldiers who had been standing there. There were no more cheers heard from the besieged Trozelligoj.

"They cower in fear!" the Hertug screamed exultantly. "Attack!"

"Not quite yet." Jason explained patiently. "You're missing the whole point of siege weapons. We do as much damage to them as we can before attacking—it helps the odds." He gave the aiming wheel a turn and the next missile bit a piece out of the wall further along. "And we change ammunition too, just to keep them on the jump."

When the stones had worked along the wall and were beginning to tear holes in the main building, Jason raised the sights a bit. "Load on a special," he ordered. These were oil-soaked bundles of rags weighted with stones and bound about with ropes.

When the special was seated in the cup he ignited it himself and did not shoot until it was burning well. The rapid journey through the air fanned it into a roaring blaze that burst expansively on the thatched roof of the enemy keep, which began immediately to crackle and smoke. "We'll try a few more of those," Jason said, happily rubbing his hands together.

The outer wall was pierced in a number of places, two towers were down, and most of the roof on fire before the desperate Trozelligoj made an attempt to strike back. Jason had been waiting for this, and noticed at once when the sea gates began to swing open.

"Cease fire," he ordered, "and keep your eyes on the pressure. I'll personally murder every one of you that survives if you let that boiler blow up." He jumped for the manned boat he had waiting alongside. "Pull for the battleship!" he said and the boat bobbed as the Hertug hurtled after him.

"The Hertug always leads!" he shouted, and almost beheaded one of the oarsmen with his wildly waving sword.

"That's all right by me," said Jason, "but just watch where you are putting that sword, and keep your head down when the shooting starts."

When Jason reached the bridge of the "Dreadnaught" he saw that the clumsy-looking Trozelligoj side-wheeler had thrashed through the sea gate and was heading directly towards them. Jason had heard blood-chilling descriptions of this powerful weapon of destruction, and he was pleased to see that it was just a ramshackle and unarmored vessel, as he had expected. "Full speed ahead," he bellowed into the speaking tube, and took the wheel himself.

The ships, head-on to each other, closed rapidly, and spears from the *jetiloj*, the oversize crossbows, rattled off the "Dreadnaught's" armor plate and splashed into the water. They did no harm and the two vessels still rushed towards each other on a collision course. The sight of the low, beetle-like and smoke-belching form of the "Dreadnaught" must have shaken the enemy captain, and he must have realized that collision at this speed could not do his ship much good, for he suddenly turned the ship away. Jason spun the wheel to follow the other, and kept his bow aimed at the ship's flank.

"Brace yourselves—we're going to hit!" he shouted as the high dragon prow of the other ship flashed past, frightened faces at the rail. Then the metal ram of the "Dreadnaught's" bow hit squarely in the middle of the dripping boards of the port paddle wheel and crashed on deep into the ship's hull. The shuddering impact hurled them from their feet as the "Dreadnaught" slammed to a stop.

"Reverse engines so we can pull free!" Jason ordered, and spun the wheel hard over.

A soldier who had jumped or been knocked from the other ship fell to the armored deck of the "Dreadnaught". Howling battle cries, the Hertug climbed out of the bridge window and attacked the dazed man, slashing him across the neck and then kicking his body into the water. Screams, thuds, and the shrill hiss of leaking steam came from the side-wheeler. The Hertug dived back to the safety of the bridge just as the first crossbow bolts slammed down from above.

The propeller whirled, full speed astern, but the "Dreadnaught" only vibrated, and did not move. Jason muttered, and threw the steering wheel hard in the opposite direction. The ship rocked and levered free, then began to move smoothly astern. Water gurgled and rushed into the holed side-wheeler, which began immediately to list and settle.

"Did you see the way I vanquished the knave who dared attack us?" the Hertug asked with immense satisfaction.

"You still swing a wicked sword," Jason told him. "Did *you* see the way I knocked a hole into that barge? Ahh! There goes the boiler," he added as a tremendous jarring thud came from the stricken enemy, followed by a cloud of steam and smoke as she broke in two and swiftly sank.

By the time Jason had swung the battleship towards their position, the side-wheeler was gone and the sea gates closed again. "Run the survivors down," the Hertug ordered, but Jason ignored him.

"There is water below," a man said, poking his head up through a hatch. "It is sloshing over our feet."

"Some of the seams opened after the crash," Jason told him. "What did you expect? This is why I installed the pumps, and we have ten extra slaves aboard. Put them to work."

"It is a day of victory," the Hertug said, looking happily at the blood on his sword. "How the swine must regret their attack on our keep!"

"They'll regret it even more before the day is over," Jason said. "We're moving into the last phase now. Are you sure that your men know what to do?"

"I have told them myself many times, and have given them the printed sheets of orders that you prepared. All is ready for the signal. When shall I give it?"

"Very soon. You stay here on the bridge, with your hand on the whistle, while I have a few more shots."

Jason transferred to the barge and planted some of the fire-bomb specials on the roof to keep the fire roaring. He followed these with a half a dozen rounds of canister shot—leather bags of fist-size stones that burst when fired—and cleared away all the firefighters and soldiers who were foolish enough to expose themselves. Then he worked the heavy stones back along the wall, crumbling it even more, until his hurtling missiles reached the sea gate. It took just four shots to batter the heavy timber into splinters and leave the gates a sagging wreck. The way was open. Jason waved his arms and jumped for the boat. The whistle screamed three times and the waiting Perssonoj vessels began to move to the attack.

Because there was no one he could trust to do an adequate job, Jason was not only commander-in-chief of the attackers, but also gun layer, artilleryman, ship's captain, and all the rest, and his legs were getting tired from running back and forth. Climbing to the bridge of the "Dreadnaught" was an effort. Once the attackers were inside the stronghold he could relax and let them finish the job in their efficiently bloodthirsty manner. He had done his part : he had weakened the defenders and caused a good number of casualties; now the forces would join in hand-to-hand combat, opening the way to complete victory.

The smaller vessels, propelled by sail and oar, were halfway to the battered walls before the "Dreadnaught" got moving, but the steam-powered battleship soon caught up with them. The attackers opened ranks and the hurtling ship plunged through, aimed directly at the drooping ruins of the sea gate. The armored bow hit, tore them screaming from their hinges, and plowed on into the pool inside. Even with full speed astern, they were making headway when they hit the dock and shuddered to a stop, with the sharp prow jammed deep into the pilings. Behind them came the roaring Perssonoj and from ahead the defending Trozelligoj, and in an instant deadly battle was joined. The Hertug's noble bodyguard were in the first wave and were waiting to protect their leader as he rushed off to the attack.

Jason slipped an emergency flask of home distillate from its padded rack and downed a stimulating dose. He poured a second one into a beaker to enjoy more slowly, and watched the battle from his vantage point on the bridge.

From the first instant that the forces met, the outcome

142

had never been in doubt. The defenders were battered, burned, and outnumbered, and they were suffering from crushed morale. They could only fall back as the Perssonoj charged over the crumbled walls and in through the open sea gate. The courtyard was swept clear and the battle moved off into the depths of the keep : it was time for Jason to do his next part.

He drained his beaker, slipped a small shield on his left arm, and grabbed up the morning star, which had proved so useful already. Ijale was somewhere in there, he was sure, and he had to find her before there were any unfortunate accidents. He felt a responsibility for the girl—she would still be walking the coastal deserts in a slave band if he hadn't come along. For better or worse, she was in this trouble because of him, and he had to get her out of it safely. He hurried ashore.

The fire in the damp thatch of the roof seemed to have gone out without causing any further damage to the stone building, but it still smoked and the halls were thick with the reek of it. In the entrance hall there was just death— bodies and blood and a few wounded. Jason kicked open a door and went deeper into the keep. A last battle was being fought by the outnumbered defenders in the main dining hall, but he skirted it and pushed through into the kitchens. Here there were only slaves cowering under the tables, and the chief cook, who attacked him with a cleaver. Jason disarmed him with a twitch of the morning star, and threatened painful death if the man didn't tell him where Ijale was. The cook talked, willingly, clutching his bloody arm, but he knew nothing. The slaves only gabbled in fear, and were hopeless, Jason pushed on.

A fearful roar of voices and a constant crashing drew him to the major remaining conflict in what was obviously the main hall, lit by tall windows and hung with flags and pennants. It was a shambles now as the warring groups surged back and forth, slipping in the blood and on the bodies of the wounded and dead. A flurry of bolts from crossbowmen at the far end of the hall drove the fighting men apart, forcing the attackers to raise their shields to defend themselves.

A line of armored and shielded men stretched across the room, and at their rear was a smaller knot of men, more gayly decorated and jeweled, undoubtedly the noble family of the Trozelligoj themselves. They were on the dining dais,

143

now swept clear of furniture, and could look over the heads of the men battling below them. One of them caught sight of Jason when he entered and pointed towards him with his sword, while talking rapidly with the others. Then they all turned their attention to him and the group opened up.

Jason saw that they held Ijale, cruelly chained and bound, and that one of them had his sword pressed to her bosom. They waved his attention to this and their meaning was obvious enough : do not attack, or she dies. They had no idea what she meant to him, or if she meant anything at all, but they must have suspected him of some affection. They were about to be slaughtered, so any desperate move was worth trying.

Jason's reaction was a roaring rage that sent him hurtling forward. Logically, he knew that there could be no compromise now; victory was at hand, and any attempt to reason with the Hertug or the desperate Perssonoj would be sure to result in Ijale's death. He must reach her !

The Trozellogoj soldiers were knocked aside as he plunged into them from the rear and flung himself on the guarding line of armored men. An arrow hurtled by, barely missing him, but unnoticed, and he was upon them. The suddenness of his attack and his charging weight drove the line back for an instant and his morning star whistled through a gap between two shields, hitting square on a helmeted face. He caught a descending sword on his shield and slammed into the man he had hit, who went down. Once past the soldiers, he did not stay to battle but pushed on, while the line tried to close to face the enemy who had rushed to take advantage of Jason's suicidal attack.

There was another member of the group on the dais whom Jason had not noticed before; he glimpsed him now as he attacked. It was Mikah, the traitor, here ! He stood next to Ijale, who was going to be murdered because Jason could not possibly reach her in time. The sword was already plunging down to slay her.

Jason had just an instant's sight of Mikah as the latter stepped forward and clutched the swordsman's shoulders and hurled him backwards to the floor. Then Jason was attacked from all sides at once and was fighting desperately for his life.

The odds were too great—five, six to one—all of the attackers armored and desperate. But he did not have to win, only to hold them off a few seconds longer until his own men arrived. They were just behind him; he could hear their victorious roar as the line of defenders went down. Jason caught one sword on his shield, kicked another attacker aside, and beat off a third with his morning star.

But there were too many. They were all about him. He thrust two aside, then turned to face the others behind him. There—the old man, the leader of these people, anger in his eyes . . . a long sword in his hands . . . thrusting.

"Die, demon! Die, destroyer!" the Trozelligoj screeched and lunged.

The long, cool blade caught Jason just above the belt, thrust into his body with a searing pain, transfixed him, emerging from his back.

CHAPTER SIXTEEN

It was pain, but it was not unbearable. What was unendurable was the sure knowledge of death. The old man had killed him. It was all over. Almost without malice, Jason raised his shield and pushed it against the man, sending him stumbling backwards. The sword remained, slim shining death through his body.

"Leave it," Jason said hoarsely to Ijale, who raised her chained hands to pull it out, her eyes numb with terror.

The battle was over, and through the blurring of pain Jason could see the Hertug before him, the awareness of death written also on his face. "Cloths," Jason said, as clearly as he could. "Have them ready to press to the wounds when the sword is removed."

Strong hands of the soldiers held him up and the cloths were ready. The Hertug stood before Jason who merely nodded and closed his eyes. Once more the pain struck at him and he fell. He was lowered to the carpet, his clothes were torn open, the flow of blood compressed beneath the waiting bandages.

As he lost consciousness, grateful for their relief from agony, he wondered why he bothered. Why prolong the pain? He could only die here, light years from antiseptics and antibiotics with destruction pushed through his guts. He could only die . . .

Jason struggled back to awareness just once to see Ijale kneeling over him with a needle and thread, sewing together the raw lips of the wound in his abdomen. The light went away again, and the next time he opened his eyes he was in his own bedroom looking at the sunlight flooding in through the broken windows. Something obscured the light, and first his forehead and his cheeks, then his lips, were moistened and cooled. It made him realize how dry his throat was and how strong the pain was.

"Water . . . ." he rasped, and was surprised at the weakness of his voice.

"It was told me that you should not drink—with a cut there," Ijale said, pointing to his body, her lips taut.

"I don't think it will matter . . . one way or the other," he told her, the knowledge of impending death more painful by far than the wound. The Hertug appeared beside Ijale, his drawn expression a mirror image of hers, and held a small box out to Jason.

"The *sciuloj* have obtained these, the roots of the *bede* that deaden pain and make it feel distant. You must chew on it. though not too much; there is great danger if too much of the *bede* is taken."

Not for me, Jason thought, forcing his jaws to chew the dry, dusty root. *A pain killer, a narcotic, a habit-forming drug . . . I'm going to have very little time to get the habit.*

Whatever the drug was, it worked fine and Jason was grateful. The pain slipped away, as did his thirst, and though he felt a little light-headed he was no longer exhausted. "How did the battle go?" he asked the Hertug, who was standing, arms folded, scowling at fate.

"Victory is ours. The only surviving Trozelligoj are our slaves; their clan has ceased to exist. Some soldiers fled, but they do not count. Their keep is ours, and the most secret chambers where they build their engines. If you could but see their machines . . ." At the realization that Jason could not see them, and would see but little else, the Hertug fell to scowling again.

"Cheer up," Jason told him. "Win one, win them all. There are no other mobs strong enough to stand up to you now. Keep moving before they can combine. Pick off the most unfriendly ones first. If possible, try not to kill all their technicians; you'll want someone to explain their secrets after you have beaten them. Move fast, and by winter you'll own Appsala."

"We'll give you the finest funeral Appsala has ever seen," the Hertug burst out.

"I'm sure of it. Spare no expense."

"There will be feasts and prayers, and your remains will be turned to ash in the electric furnace in the honor of the god Elektro."

"Nothing could make me happier . . ."

"And afterwards they will be taken to sea at the head of a magnificent funeral procession, ship after ship, all of them heavily armed so that on the return voyage we can fall on the Mastreguloj and take them unawares."

"That's more like it, Hertug. I thought for a while there that you were getting too sentimental."

A crashing at the door drew Jason's attention, and he turned his head, slowly, to see a group of slaves dragging heavily insulated cables into the room. Others carried boxes of equipment, and behind them came the slave overseer cracking his whip, driving Mikah's tottering, chained figure before him. Mikah was booted into a corner, where he collapsed.

"I was going to kill the traitor," the Hertug said, "until I thought how nice it would be for you to torture him to death yourself. You'll enjoy that. The arc furnace will be hot soon and you can cook him bit by bit, send him ahead as a sacrifice to Elektro to smooth the way for your coming."

"That's very considerate of you," Jason said, eyeing Mikah's battered form. "Chain him to the wall, then leave us, so that I may think of the most ingenious and terrible tortures for him."

"I shall do as you ask. But you must let me watch the ceremony. I am always interested in something new in torture."

"I'm sure you are, Hertug."

They left, and Jason saw Ijale stalking Mikah with the kitchen knife.

"Don't do it," Jason told her. "It's no good, no good at all."

She obediently put the knife down, and took up the sponge to wipe Jason's face. Mikah lifted his head and looked at Jason. His face was bruised, and one eye was puffed shut.

"Would you tell me," Jason asked, "just what in hell you thought you were doing by betraying us and trying to get me captured by the Trozelligoj?"

"Though you torture me, my lips are eternally shut."

"Don't be a bigger idiot than usual. No one's going to torture you. I just wonder what you had in mind this time—what ever led you to pull this kind of stunt?"

"I did what I thought best," Mikah answered, drawing himself up.

"You *always* do what you think best—only you usually think wrong. Didn't you like the way I treated you?"

"There was nothing personal in what I did. It was for the good of suffering mankind."

"I think you did it for the reward and a new job, and because you were angry at me," Jason needled, knowing Mikah's weaknesses.

"Never! If you must know . . . I did it to prevent war. . . ."

"Just what do you mean by that?"

Mikah scowled, looking ominous and judicial in spite of his battered eye. His chains rattled as he pointed an accusing finger at Jason.

"Deep in drink one day you did confess your crime to me, and did speak of your plans to wage deadly war among these innocent people, to embroil them in slaughter and to set cruel despotism about their necks. I knew then what I had to do. You had to be stopped. I forced my lips shut, not daring to say a word lest I reveal my thoughts, because I knew a way.

"I had been approached by a man in the hire of the Trozelligoj, a clan of honest laborers and mechanics, he assured me, who wished to hire you away from the Perssonoj at a good wage. I did not answer him at the time, because any plan to free us would involve violence and loss of life, and I could not consider this even though refusing meant my remaining in chains. Then, when I learned of your bloodthirsty intentions. I examined my conscience and saw what had to be done. We would all be removed from here, taken to the Trozelligoj, who promised that no harm would come to you, though you would be kept a prisoner. The war would be averted."

"You are a simple fool," Jason said, without passion. Mikah flushed.

"I do not care what your opinion is of me. I would act the same again if there was the opportunity."

"Even though you now know that the mob you were selling out to are no better than the ones here? Didn't you stop one of them from killing Ijale during the fighting? I suppose I should thank you for that—even though you are the one who got her into the spot."

"I do not want your thanks. It was the passion of the moment that made them threaten her. I cannot blame them. . . ."

"It doesn't matter one way or the other. The war is over; they lost, and my plans for an industrial revolution will go through without a hitch, even without my personal attention. About the only thing you have accomplished is to bring about my death—which I find very hard to forgive."

"What madness. . .?"

"*Madness*, you narrow-minded fool!" Jason pushed himself up on one arm, but had to drop back as an arrow of pain shot through the muffling layers of the drug. "Do you think I'm lying here because I'm tired? Your kidnaping and intriguing led me a lot further into battle than I ever intended, and right onto a long, sharp, unsanitary sword. It stuck me like a pig."

"I don't understand what you are saying."

"Then you are being very dim. I was run through, front to back. My knowledge of anatomy is not as good as it might be, but at at guess I would say no organ of vital importance was penetrated. If my liver or any major blood vessels had been punctured, I wouldn't be talking to you now. But I don't know of any way to make a hole through the abdomen without cutting a loop or two of intestine, slicing up the peritoneum and bringing in a lot of nice hungry bacteria. In case you haven't read the first-aid book lately, what happens next is an infection called peritonitis, which, considering the medical knowledge on this planet, is one hundred per cent fatal."

This shut Mikah up nicely, but it didn't cheer Jason very much, so he closed his eyes for a little rest. When he opened them again it was dark and he dozed on and off until dawn, when he had to wake Ijale to tell her to bring him the bowl of *bede* roots. She wiped his forehead and he noticed the expression on her face.

"Then it's not getting hotter in here," he said. "It's me."

"You were hurt because of me," Ijale wailed, and she began to cry.

"Nonsense!" Jason told her. "No matter what way I die, it will be suicide. I settled that a long time ago. On the planet where I was born there was nothing but sunny days and endless peace and a long, long life. I decided to leave, preferring a short, full one to a long and empty one. Now let's have a bit more of that root to chew on, because I would like to forget my troubles."

The drug was powerful, and the infection was deep. Jason drifted along sinking into the reddish fog of the *bede*, then coming back up out of it to find nothing changed. Ijale was still there, tending him, Mikah in the far corner brooding in

150

his chains. He wondered what would happen to them when he died, and the thought troubled him.

It was during one of these black, conscious moods that he heard the sound, a growing rumble that suddenly cracked the air outside, then died away. He levered himself up onto his elbows, heedless of the pain, and shouted.

"Ijale, where are you? Come here at once!"

She ran from the other room, and he was conscious of shouts outside, voices on the canal, in the courtyard. Had he really heard it? Or was it a feverish hallucination? Ijale was trying to force him down, but he shrugged her away and called to Mikah. "Did you hear anything just then? Did you hear it?"

"I was asleep—I think I heard . . ."

"*What?*"

"A roar—it woke me up. It sounded like . . . but it is impossible . . ."

"Impossible? Why impossible? It was a rocket engine, wasn't it? Here on this primitive planet."

"But there are no rockets here."

"There are now, you idiot. Why do you think I built my radio-broadcasting prayer wheel?" He frowned in sudden thought, trying to cudgel his fogged and fevered brain into action.

"Ijale," he called, rooting under his pillow for the purse concealed there. "Take this money—all of it—and get down to the Temple of Elektro and give it to the priests. Don't let anyone stop you, because this is the most important thing you have ever done. They have probably stopped grinding the wheel and have all gone outside for a look at the excitement. That rocket will never find the right spot without a guide beam—and if it lands any place else in Appsala there could be trouble. Tell them to crank, and not to stop cranking, because a ship of the gods is on the way here and it needs all the prayers it can get."

She ran out and Jason sank back, breathing rapidly. Was it a spaceship out there that had picked up his S.O.S.? Would it have a doctor or a medical machine that could cure him at this advanced stage of infection? It must have, every ship carried some medical provision. For the first time since he had been wounded he allowed himself to believe that there might be a chance he could survive, and a black weight lifted from him. He even managed a smile at Mikah.

"I have a feeling, Mikah old son, that we have eaten our last *kreno*. Do you think you can bear up under that burden?"

"I will be forced to turn you in," Mikah said gravely. "Your crimes are too serious to conceal; I cannot do otherwise. I must tell the captain to notify the police . . ."

"How did a man with your kind of mind live this long?" Jason asked coldly. "What's to stop me from having you killed and buried right now so that you could make no charges?"

"I do not think you would do that. You are not without a certain kind of honor."

" 'Certain kind of honor'! A word of praise from you! Can it be possible that there is the tiniest of chinks in the rock-ribbed fastness of your mind?"

Before Mikah could answer the roar of the rocket returned, coming lower and not dying away as before, but growing louder instead, becoming deafening, and a shadow moved across the sun.

"Chemical rockets!" Jason shouted over the noise. "A pinnance or landing boat from a spacer . . . it must be zeroing in on my spark radio—there's no possibility of coincidence here." At that moment Ijale ran into the room and hurled herself down by Jason's bed.

"The priests have fled," she wailed; "everyone is in hiding. A great fire-breathing beast has come down to destroy us all!" Her voice was suddenly a shout as the roar in the courtyard outside stopped.

"It's down safely," Jason breathed, then pointed to his drawing materials on the table. "The paper and a pencil, Ijale. Let me have them. I'm going to write a note that I want you to take down to the ship that landed." She recoiled, shivering.

"You mustn't be afraid, Ijale, it's just a ship like the ones that you have been in, only one made to sail in the air rather than on the water. It will have people in it who won't harm you. Go out and show them this note, then bring them here."

"I am afraid . . ."

"Don't be; no harm will come of this. The people in the ship will help me, and I think they can make me well again."

"Then I go," she said simply, rising and forcing herself, still shaking, out of the door.

Jason watched her leave. "There are times, Mikah," he

152

said, "when I'm not looking at you, that I can be proud of the human race."

The minutes stretched out and Jason found himself pulling at the blankets, twisting them with his fingers, wondering what was happening outside in the courtyard. He started as there was a sudden clanging on metal, followed immediately by a rapid series of explosions. Were the fools attacking the ship? He writhed and cursed at his own weakness when he tried to get up. All he could do was lie there and wait— while his existence lay in others' hands.

More explosions sounded—inside the building this time —as well as shouts and a loud scream. Running footsteps came down the hall and Ijale hurried in and Meta, gun still smoking in her hand, entered behind her.

"It's a long way from Pyrrus," Jason said, resting his eyes on the troubled beauty of her face, on the familiar woman's body in the harsh metalcloth suit. "But I can't think of anyone I would rather see come through that door. . . ."

"You're hurt!" She ran swiftly to him, kneeling on the far side of the bed so that she still faced the open door. When she took up his hand her eyes widened at the dry heat of his skin. She said nothing, but unclipped the medikit from her belt and pressed it against the skin of his forearm. The analyzing probe pushed down and it clicked busily, injecting him with one hypodermic needle, then with three more in rapid succession. It buzzed a bit more, then gave him a swift vaccination and switched on the "treatment completed" light.

Meta's face was close above his; she bent a little nearer and kissed him on his cracked lips and a curl of golden hair fell forward, and she kissed him with her eyes open, and without even pulling away fired a shot that blew out a corner of the door frame and drove back the soldiers in the hall.

"Don't shoot them," Jason said, when she had reluctantly drawn away. "They're supposed to be friends."

"Not my friends. As soon as I left the lifeboat they fired on me with some sort of primitive projectile weapon, but I took care of that. They even fired at the girl who brought your message, until I blew one of the walls down. Are you feeling better?"

"Neither good nor bad, just dizzy from the shots you gave me. But we had better get to the ship. I'll see if I can walk."

He threw his legs over the edge of the bed and collapsed, face down on the floor. Meta dragged him back onto the bed and arranged the blankets over him again.

"You must stay here until you are better. You are too sick to move now."

"I'll be a lot sicker if I stay. As soon as the Hertug—he's the one in charge here—realizes that I may be leaving, he will do anything to keep me here, no matter how many men he loses doing it. We are going to have to move before his evil little mind reaches that conclusion."

Meta was looking around the room, and her glance slid over Ijale—who was crouched down staring at her—as if she were part of the furnishings, then stopped at Mikah. "Is that creature chained to the wall dangerous?" she asked.

"At times he can be; you have to keep a close eye on him. He's the one who seized me on Pyrrus."

Meta's hand flew to a pouch at her waist and she slipped an extra gun into Jason's hand. "Here is a gun—you will want to kill him yourself."

"See, Mikah," Jason said, feeling the familiar weight of the weapon in his palm. "Everyone wants me to kill you. What is there about you that makes everyone loathe you so?"

"I am not afraid to die," Mikah said, raising his head and squaring his shoulders, but not looking very impressive with his scraggly grey beard and the chains he wore.

"Well, you should be." Jason lowered the gun. "It's surprising that someone with your passion for doing the wrong thing has lasted this long."

He turned to Meta. "I've had enough of killing for a while," he told her; "this planet is steeped in it. And we'll need him to help carry me downstairs, I don't think I can make it on my own, and he's probably the best stretcher bearer we can find."

Meta turned towards Mikah and her gun shot from its power holster into her hand and fired. He recoiled, raising his arm before his eyes, then seemed shocked to find himself still alive. Meta had freed him by shooting his chains away. She slid over to him with the effortless grace of a stalking tiger and pushed the still smoking muzzle of her gun deep into his midsection.

"Jason doesn't want me to kill you," she purred, and twisted the gun a bit deeper, "but I don't always do what he tells me. If you want to live a while you will do what *I* say. You will take the top off that table to make a stretcher. You will help carry Jason on it down to the rocket. Cause any kind of trouble, and you will be dead. Do you understand?"

Mikah opened his mouth for a protest, or perhaps for one of his speeches, but something in the icy bitterness of the girl stayed him. He merely nodded and turned to the table.

Ijale was crouched next to Jason's bed now, holding tight to his hand. She had not understood a word of any of the off-world languages they had spoken.

"What is happening, Jason?" she pleaded. "What was the shiny thing that bit your arm? This new one kissed you, so she must be your woman, but you are strong and can have two women. Do not leave me."

"Who is the girl?" Meta asked coldly. Her power holster buzzed and the muzzle of her gun slipped in and out.

"One of the locals, a slave who helped me," Jason said with an offhandedness he did not feel. "If we leave her here they will probably kill her. She'll come with us. . . ."

"I don't think that is wise." Meta's eyes were slitted, and her gun seemed about to leap into her hand. A Pyrran woman in love was still a woman—and still a Pyrran, a terribly dangerous combination. Luckily a stir at the door distracted her and she blasted two shots in that direction before Jason could stop her.

"Hold it—that's the Hertug. I recognized his heels as he dived for safety."

A frightened voice quavered from the hall. "We did not know this one was your friend, Jason. Some soldiers, too enthusiastic, shot too soon. I have had them punished. We are friends, Jason. Tell the one from the ship not to make more of the blowing-up, so that I can enter and talk to you."

"I do not understand his words," Meta said, "but I don't like the sound of his voice."

"Your instincts are perfectly right, darling," Jason told her. "He couldn't be more two-faced if he had eyes, nose, and mouth on the back of his head."

Jason chuckled, and realized he was getting light-headed with all the battling drugs and toxins in his system. Clear thinking was an effort, but it was an effort that had to be made. They still weren't out of trouble and, as good a fighter as Meta was, she couldn't be expected to beat an entire army. And that's what would be called out to stop them if he didn't watch his step.

"Come on in, Hertug," he called out. "No one will hurt you—these mistakes happen." And then to Meta : "Don't shoot—but don't relax either. I'll try to talk him out of causing trouble, but I can't guarantee it, so stand ready for anything."

The Hertug took a quick look in the door and bobbed out of sight again. He finally rallied the remains of his nerve and shuffled in hesitantly.

"That's a nice little weapon your friend has, Jason. Tell him"—he blinked nearsighted eyes at Meta's uniform—"I mean her, that we'll trade some slaves for one. Five slaves, that's a good bargain."

"Say seven."

"Agreed. Hand it over."

"Not this one; it has been in her family for years and she couldn't bear to part with it. But there is another one in the ship she arrived in—we'll go down and get it."

Mikah had finished dismembering the table and he laid the top of it next to Jason's bed; then he and Meta slid Jason carefully onto it. The Hertug wiped his nose with the back of his hand, and his blinking red eyes took everything in.

"In the ship there are things that will make you well," he said, showing more intelligence than Jason had given him credit for. "You will not die, and you will leave in the sky ship?"

Jason groaned and writhed on the stretcher, clutching at his side in agony. "I'm dying, Hertug! They take my ashes to the ship, a space-going funeral barge, to scatter them among the stars—"

The Hertug dived for the doorway, but Meta was on him in the same instant, swinging his arm up behind his back until he screamed, and digging her gun into his kidneys.

"What are your plans, Jason?" she asked calmly.

"Let Mikah carry the front of the stretcher, and the Hertug and Ijale can hold up the back. Keep the old boy under your gun, and with a little luck we'll get out of here with whole skins."

They went out that way, slowly and carefully. The leaderless Perssonoj could not make up their minds what to do; the pained shouts from the Hertug only rattled them, as did

Jason's shots, which blasted chunks of masonry and blew out windows. He enjoyed the trip down the stairs and across the courtyard, and cheered himself by putting a shot near any head that appeared. They reached the rocket without difficulty.

"Now comes the hard part," Jason said, wrapping an arm about Ijale's shoulders and throwing most of his weight on the other arm, clutched on Mikah's neck. He couldn't walk, but they could hold him up and drag him aboard. "Stay in the door, Meta, with a firm grip on the old buzzard. Expect anything to happen, because there is no such thing as loyalty here, and if they have to kill the Hertug to get you they won't hesitate for an instant."

"That is logical," Meta agreed. "After all, it is war."

"Yes, I suppose a Pyrran would look at it that way. Stand ready. I'll warm the engines, and when we're ready to take off I'll blow the siren. Drop the Hertug, close the lock, and get to the controls as fast as you can—I don't think I could manage a takeoff. Understand?"

"Perfectly. Go—you are wasting time."

Jason slumped in the co-pilot's seat and ran through the starting cycle as fast as he could. He was just reaching for the siren button when there was a jarring thump and the whole ship shook, and—for one heart-stopping second—it rocked and almost fell over. It slowly righted itself and he hit the alarm. Before it stopped echoing, Meta was in the pilot's seat and the little rocket blasted skywards.

"They are more advanced than I thought they would be on this primitive world," she said, as soon as the first thrust of acceleration eased. "There was a great, ugly machine in one of the buildings that suddenly smoked and threw a rock that took most of our port fin away. I blew it up, but the one you call the Hertug escaped."

"In some ways they are very advanced," Jason said, feeling too weak to admit that they had been almost finished off by his own invention.

CHAPTER SEVENTEEN

With Meta's skilful piloting, they slid easily into the open hold of the Pyrran spacer that was orbiting just outside the atmosphere. Being in free fall eased Jason's pain enough for him to make sure that the wide-eyed and terrorized Ijale was strapped into an acceleration couch before he collapsed. After that he floated towards a bunk himself, and before he reached it passed out with a happy smile: the slave-holding monomaniacs already seemed far behind.

When he awoke much of the pain and discomfort was gone, as well as the fever; and though he was dreadfully weak he was able to pull himself through the passageway to the control room. Meta was plotting a course on the computer.

"Food!" Jason croaked, clutching at his throat. "My tissues exhaust themselves making repairs and I starve."

Meta wordlessly passed him a squeeze-flask dinner, managing to do it in such a way that he knew she was angry about something. As he put the tube in his mouth he saw Ijale crouched on the far side of the compartment—at least, crouching as much as she was capable of in free fall.

"My, that was good!" Jason exclaimed with false joviality. "Are you flying this ship alone, Meta?"

"Of course I'm alone." She said it in such a way that it sounded more like: *Aren't you a fool?* "I was allowed to take the ship, but no one could be spared to go with me."

"How did you find me?" he asked, trying to discover a subject that she might warm to.

"That should be obvious. The operator at the spaceport noted the insignia when the spacer left with you in it, and when he described it Kerk recognized it as Cassylian. I went to Cassylia and investigated; they identified the ship, but there was no record of it having returned. Then I followed a reverse course to Pyrrus and found three possible planets near enough to the course to have registered in the ship during jump-space flight. Two of them are centrally organized, with modern spaceports and flight controls, and would have known if the ship I was seeking had landed, or even crashed. It hadn't. Therefore the ship must have landed on the third one, the planet we have just left. As soon as I entered the atmosphere I heard the distress signal and came as fast as I could. . . . What are you going to do with that woman?"

These last words were spoken in an icy tone. Ijale crouched lower, not understanding a word of the conversation, but obviously petrified with fear.

"I haven't really thought about it yet . . ."

"There is only room for one woman in your life, Jason. Me. I'll kill anyone who thinks differently."

Without a doubt she meant it; and if Ijale was going to live much longer she had to be separated as quickly as possible from the deadly threat of female-Pyrran jealousy. Jason thought fast.

"We'll stop at the next civilized planet and let her off. I have enough money to leave a deposit in a bank that will last her for years. And I'll make arrangements for it to be paid out only a bit at a time, so no matter how she is cheated she will always have enough. I'm not going to worry about her—if she was able to live in the *kreno* legion she can get along anywhere on a settled world."

He could already hear the complaints that would come when he broke the news to Ijale, but it was for her own survival.

"I shall care for her and lead her in the paths of righteousness," a remembered voice spoke from the doorway. Mikah stood there, clutching at the jamb, bushy-bearded and bright-eyed.

"That's a wonderful idea!" Jason agreed enthusiastically. He turned to Ijale and spoke to her in her own language. "Did you hear that? Mikah is going to take you home with him and look after you. I'll arrange for some money to be paid to you for all your needs—he'll explain to you all about money. I want you to listen to him carefully, note exactly what he says, then do the exact opposite. You must promise me you will do that, and never break your word. In that way, though you may make some mistakes, and will sometimes be wrong, the rest of the time things will go very smoothly."

"I cannot leave you! Take me with you—I'll be your slave always!" she wailed.

"What did she say?" Meta snapped, catching some of the meaning.

"You are evil, Jason," Mikah declaimed, getting the needle back into the familiar groove. "She will obey you, I know that, no matter how I labor she will ayways do as you say."

"I sincerely hope so," Jason said fervently. "One has to be born into your particular brand of illogic to get any pleasure from it. The rest of us are happier bending a bit under the impact of existence, and exacting a mite more pleasure from the physical life around us."

"Evil I say, and you shall not go unpunished." Mikah's hand appeared from behind the door jamb, and it held a pistol that he had found below. "I am taking command of this ship. You will secure the two women so that they can cause no trouble; then we will proceed to Cassylia for your trial."

Meta had her back turned to Mikah and was sitting in the control chair a good five meters from him, her hands filled with navigational notes. She slowly raised her head and looked at Jason and a smile broke across her face.

"You said you didn't want him killed."

"I still don't want him killed, but I also have no intention of going to Cassylia." He echoed her smile, and turned away.

He sighed happily, and there was a sudden rush of feet behind his back. No shots were fired, but a hoarse scream, a thud, and a sharp cracking noise told him that Mikah had lost his last argument.